SEXUAL

HARASSMENT

Speaking Out And Standing Up!

Dr. Derrick Martin

SEXUAL HARASSMENT

Table of Contents

INTRODUCTION

Sexual harassment is a problem that has existed in various organizations around the world since they were established. It became publicly acknowledged about three decades ago as a big issue that requires serious intervention. It takes different forms and can happen in diverse contexts. Sexual harassment is not limited to certain environments. It's a negative social phenomenon that can be experienced by anyone, regardless of their gender or age.

The term sexual harassment refers to behavior that demeans, humiliates or derogates a person based on their gender. Such behavior may comprise sexual force and degradation, sexist comments, jokes, materials or other acts an individual experiences because of their gender. These acts can threaten, ridicule, sabotage or undermine them.

Sometimes, sex-based harassment does not appear sexual in nature. Some kinds of harassment like endangerment or sabotage could have little or nothing to do with gender but are still targeted towards an individual because of their gender.

Sexual harassment can be psychologically harmful when it threatens an individual's well-being. For example, it can have negative psychological effects like anxiety or depression. Harassment can even reduce self-esteem, confidence, and self-worth. An experience of sexual harassment can either trigger symptoms of depression and anxiety that are new to the person, or it can worsen a previous condition that may have been suppressed or resolved. Victims may notice a worsening of symptoms. It has been observed that sexual harassment early in one's career, in particular, can cause long-term depressive symptoms.

A person going through or dealing with the aftermath of sexual harassment may also exhibit symptoms of Post-traumatic disorder, especially if the harassment leads to violence and/or assault.

Among women who experience sexual assault, 90 percent who experience sexual violence in the immediate aftermath have symptoms of acute stress. For most people, these symptoms fade over time through social support and coping strategies, and many people totally recover and move on with normal life. Still, others become distressed that the experience seriously interferes with their work and personal life. It takes a certain number of symptoms to diagnose the real issue, but at that point, it's most likely to become PTSD.

Although men also experience sexual harassment, they may be more reluctant to report such encounters than women. There are a number of possible reasons for this – stigma is one of the main factors. Many men may be too embarrassed to report sexual harassment, or they may think its "unmanly" to report such an ordeal.

Sexual harassment was first recognized in cases whereby women lost their jobs because they turned down sexual overtures from their employers. This type of sexual harassment became referred to as quid pro quo sexual harassment (Latin for "this for that," meaning that getting a job or educational opportunity depended on some kind of sexual performance.) This coercive behavior was judged to constitute a violation of Title VII of the 1964 Civil Rights Act.

Later on, it was observed in employment law that pervasive sexist behavior from coworkers can create unfavorable conditions of employment—what became defined as a hostile work environment—and also constituted illegal discrimination.

Hostile work or educational environments can be triggered by actions like addressing women in crude or objectifying terms, posting pornographic images in the workplace, and by making demeaning or derogatory statements about women, such as telling anti-female jokes. Hostile environment harassment also comprises offensive and unwanted sexual behaviors such as exposing one's genitals, stroking and kissing someone and pressuring a person to go on dates even if no quid pro quo is involved.

The main distinction between quid pro quo and hostile environment harassment is that quid pro quo typically involves a one-on-one relationship in which the perpetrator has authority over employment or educational-related rewards or punishments over the target. On the other hand, hostile environment harassment can involve many perpetrators and many targets. In the hostile environment form of sexual harassment, coworkers usually display a pattern of hostile sexist behavior toward multiple targets over a long period of time.

For hostile sex-related or gender-related behavior to be considered illegal sexual harassment, it must be pervasive or severe enough to be acknowledged as having had an adverse impact upon the work or educational environment. That means isolated or single occurrences of such behavior typically qualify only when they are concluded to be sufficiently severe. Legal scholars and judges have continued to use the two subtype definitions of quid pro quo and hostile environment to describe sexual harassment.

Illegal sexual harassment is listed under the umbrella of a more comprehensive category known as discriminatory behavior. Illegal discrimination can occur based on any legally protected category: race, ethnicity, religious creed, age, sex, gender identity, marital status, national origin, ancestry, sexual orientation, genetic information, physical or mental disabilities, veteran status, prior conviction of a crime, gender identity, orientation or expression, or membership in other protected classes recognized in state or federal law.

Gender harassment is a term coined to emphasize that harmful or illegal sexual harassment does not have to be based on sexual activity. Sexual harassment encompasses discrimination because it is harmful and it's based on gender—it is not necessarily driven by sexual desire. It doesn't necessarily involve sexual activity.

Both legal doctrine and social science research acknowledge gender as comprising both one's biological sex and gender-based stereotypes and expectations, like heterosexuality and proper performance of gender roles. Sexual harassment in the form of gender harassment can be based on the violation of cultural gender stereotypes. For instance, a man may become a victim of gender harassment for being a "sissy" or being easily embarrassed by pornography. This reaction might be considered as violating stereotypes that men should be strong, heterosexual, and sexually bold.

Gender harassment is the most common type of sexual harassment. It refers to "a broad range of verbal and nonverbal behaviors not aimed at sexual cooperation but that exhibit insulting, hostile, and degrading attitudes about" members of a particular gender. Gender harassment is further defined by two types: sexist hostility and crude harassment.

For instance, a woman may be gender harassed for choosing a job traditionally held by a man or in a traditionally male field. Gender harassment in such a situation might consist of actions to sabotage the woman's equipment, machinery, or tools, or telling the woman she is not intelligent enough for scientific work.

Examples of the sexist hostility form of gender harassment for women include demeaning jokes or comments about women, comments that women do not deserve leadership positions or are not smart enough to have a successful scientific career, and sabotaging women. The crude harassment form of gender harassment is defined as the use of sexually crude terms that undermine people based on their gender.

Both women and men can and do experience all three forms of sexual harassment, but some subgroups encounter higher rates of harassment than others. For example, women who are lesbian or bisexual, women who endorse gender-egalitarian beliefs and women who are stereotypically masculine in behavior, appearance, or personality experience sexual harassment at higher rates than other women. Similarly, men who are gay, transgender, petite, or in some way perceived as "not man enough" face more harassment than other men.

Sexual harassment against men has mostly occurred in educational environments before advancing to working life. In both middle school and high school in the US, there is evidence to show that boys can experience high levels of sexual harassment. Boys are especially likely to be victims of verbal sexual harassment.

One credible finding across the evidence on male sexual harassment is that it can have a devastating impact on mental health. Men who have been sexually harassed are more likely to experience high levels of anxiety, depression and often resort to alcohol abuse. This can consequently lead to education and employment problems, such as dropping out of school, being fired or quitting work and low morale. For many male survivors, stereotypes about masculinity can further make it hard to disclose to friends, family, or the community. Men and boys may face challenges understanding that it is possible for them to be victims of sexual harassment, especially if the perpetrator is a woman.

Sexual harassment is socially harassing when it undermines, demeans or ridicules an individual in the eyes of others. It is illegally grassing when it affects a person's employment, unreasonably decreases productivity, work performance or creates a hostile, offensive and intimidating work environment.

Although sexual harassment was initially thought to be mostly perpetrated by male supervisors whose victims were mainly female subordinates, recent incidents have shown that harassment is also perpetrated by coworkers.

In service-based industries, sexual harassment is commonly perpetrated by customers. And when men are harassed, they are harassed as or more often by men as by women.

When considering organizational and group contexts, the prevalence of sexual-based harassment in the Armed Forces, and the Departments of State, Transportation, Treasury, and Justice, is 15 percent higher than in other agencies. A 2003 meta-analysis found that sexual-based harassment was highest in military samples (69%), followed by academic samples at 58 %, the private sector at 46% and government at 43%.

Industry-specific norms slightly differ. For example, Wall Street firms have experienced several sex discrimination suits since the late 90s. Harassment rates also vary by workgroup within organizations. It is more common in workgroups that report tolerance by management and less common in organizations where harassment is punished.

Sexual-based harassment rates are also influenced by certain factors, collectively known as job gender context. This includes the gender ratio of one's workgroup and the degree to which one's profession has been traditionally dominated by men or women. The gender of the supervisor is also the main factor. Bigger work groups report higher rates of harassment than smaller ones, with cases of interpersonal difficulties in bigger groups.

Since the last half-century, movements with a mission to eliminate sexual violence have challenged cultural norms about violence against women, increased awareness, and influenced significant legal and policy changes. The landmark Violence Against Women Act alone, enacted in 1994 and renewed three times since, stiffened criminal penalties against perpetrators, offered services and support channels for survivors, and established coordinated systems to prevent and respond to violence against women.

With the shift from #MeToo to Time's Up, movement leaders are strategically defining sexual violence as a social and cultural menace, rather than an individual problem. This approach helps people reflect on the diverse range of actions that can be taken to systemically prevent sexual violence.

Scholars and advocates are confident that movements like these will accomplish even greater social change. This optimism stems from what has been perceived as a significant shift in the national conversation about sexual violence, from #MeToo to Time's Up.

The #MeToo hashtag has brought to public attention to the prevalence of sexual violence in ways that data alone has not achieved. For a long time, advocates have given worrying statistics, (for instance, one in five US women will be raped in her lifetime, another American is sexually assaulted every 98 seconds and many others) —with the expectation that these numbers would mobilize action. The #MeToo hashtag's popularity has made people understand what they couldn't from single data points: the actual number of women and men who have gone through some form of sexual violence in their lifetimes.

In 2006, Tarana Burke, an activist, and survivor, founded the #MeToo movement to achieve "empowerment through empathy" among those who have experienced abuse, especially women and girls of color. The movement—and its phenomenal hashtag—went viral in 2017, inspiring millions of women and men around the world to tell their stories of abuse, eventually leading to the public downfall of many powerful men.

In response to MeToo came Time's Up, an initiative that connects those who experience sexual abuse with assistance regarding legal and public relations. Inspired by activist female farmworkers, Time's Up founders define it as a "first step" towards eliminating the systemic inequities that underlie sexual violence. Such inequities include involving women in decision-making and acknowledging women in powerful positions.

Time's Up is focusing on sexual violence that happens in the workplace. This gives advocates an opportunity to broaden the national conversation beyond individuals and explain how systems shape violence.

Sexual violence exists not only in the hearts and minds of people who commit violence but also in the places where we work and live. It comes from, is exacerbated by, and is allowed to thrive in workplace cultures that systematically rob women of agency, autonomy, and decision-making power. Institutions, rather than individuals, are the target of this movement's social change strategy.

The solution is not limited to punishing harassers but rather to helping file legal claims against those who commit violence and holding the institutions that support them accountable. Located at the National Women's Law Center, Time's Up's defense fund offers survivors access to fast and comprehensive legal and communications assistance that will empower individuals and help facilitate long-term systemic change.

The biggest predictors of the occurrence of sexual harassment are organizational. Individual-level factors like sexist attitudes, beliefs that rationalize or justify harassment, that might make someone decide to harass a work colleague, student, or peer are also important. Still, a person who has proclivities for sexual harassment will have those behaviors highly inhibited when interacting with role models who behave in a professional way as compared with role models who behave in a harassing way, or when in an environment that does not tolerate harassing behaviors and/or has strong consequences for these behaviors.

Women working in environments where men outnumber women, leadership is male-dominated, and/or jobs or occupations are considered atypical for women face more frequent occurrences of sexual harassment. When comparing women who work in gender-balanced workgroups, that is equal numbers of men and women in the workgroup with those who work with almost all men, women in the latter category were 1.68 times more likely to experience gender harassment.

Hierarchical work environments like the military, where there is a significant power differential between organizational levels and an expectation is not to question those in higher positions typically have higher rates of sexual harassment than organizations that have less power differential between the organizational levels, like the private sector and government.

Environments that permit drinking during work breaks and have permissive norms related to drinking are positively associated with higher levels of gender harassment of women. Culturally, these trends are more common in currently or historically male-dominated workplaces.

The historical and cultural context of a work or education environment is of high importance to the study of sexual harassment as well, since settings or environments that are no longer male-dominated in gender ratio may still be male-dominated in other aspects like work practices, culture, or behavioral expectations.

The perceived absence of organizational sanctions accelerates the risk of sexual harassment perpetration. Perceptions of organizational tolerance for sexual harassment (also referred to as organizational climate for sexual harassment), are classified into three categories: (1) the perceived risk to targets for complaining, (2) a perceived lack of sanctions against offenders, and (3) the presumption that one's complaints will not be taken seriously.

Specifically, the more male-dominated the work environment, the more women encounter the gender harassment form of sexual harassment.

Research has concluded that perceptions of an organization's tolerance for all three forms of sexually harassing behavior are significantly related to both direct and ambient sexual harassment. In settings that are considered as more tolerant or permissive of sexual harassment, women are more likely to be directly harassed and to witness harassment of others. One meta-analysis that combined data from 41 studies with a total sample size of nearly 70,000 respondents found a perception of organizational tolerance to be the most significant predictor of sexual harassment in work organizations. In a 2017 national survey of 615 working men sexually harassing behavior was more commonly reported among men who say their company has not drawn up guidelines against harassment, hotlines to report it or sanctions for perpetrators, or who believe their managers don't care.

In one study, college men who had exhibited a willingness to sexually coerce were found to be more likely to sexually exploit a female trainee when they were exposed to an authority figure who acted in a sexually exploitive way. A 2009 study found that viewing a sexist film provoked the tendency among the less sexist men to perform acts of gender harassment. In another experiment, men who watched sexist TV clips were more likely to send women unsolicited sexist jokes and more likely to exhibit a willingness to get involved in sexual coercion than men who watched programs portraying young, successful women in domains such as science, culture, and business.

Social situations in which sexist views and sexually harassing behavior are modeled can enable, enhance, or even encourage sexually harassing behaviors, while, on the contrary, positive role models can prevent sexually harassing behavior.

Conversely, experiments indicate that sexual harassment is less likely to occur if those behaviors are not accepted by powerful and authoritative figures.

This book explores sexual harassment using an in-depth approach, one that explains the various forms of harassment, its causes, impact and how it can be prevented through proper intervention.

CHAPTER ONE: THE DEFINITION OF SEXUAL HARASSMENT

Sexual harassment is one of the major social problems which has been highly prevalent for decades. Despite receiving intense concern and extensive investigation, this problem remains an immoral behavior in a modern global society.

Sexual harassment refers to unwanted sexual advances, requests for sexual favors, and other physical or verbal expressions of a sexual nature that intimidate or humiliate a specific person or group.

Harassment involves various actions, from mild provocations to sexual abuse or assault. It can take place in different social settings like the workplace, schools, homes, churches and many others. All genders are likely to experience sexual harassment. Victims of offenders can be of any gender.

Sexual harassment is illegal in most modern legal settings. Laws regarding sexual harassment don't generally criminalize irritating comments, teasing or minor isolated occurrences because they don't impose a general civility code. In the workplace, harassment is termed as   illegal when it is persistent or severe, consequently encouraging an unfavorable and hostile work environment; or when it leads to an unfair employment decision like the victim's demotion, dismissal or quitting.

Harassment can occur when:

• The advances are made as terms for an individual's education, employment, living environment or involvement in a learning institution.

• The acceptance or declination of such advances is then used as the basis in making decisions that affect an individual's employment, education, living environment, or participation in a certain institution.

• The harassment adversely affects an individual's academic or employment performance or creates an intimidating, harsh or offensive environment for that individual's education, employment, living environment, or participation in a learning institution.

Other forms of harassment include:

• Verbal harassment that involves jokes associated with sexual orientation or sexual acts.

• Discussion of sexual relations, fantasies or stories in inappropriate places like work, school or other places.

• Being pressured to have sexual relations with someone.

• Unwanted photos, videos, emails or text messages that are sexually explicit.

Mostly, the harasser is more powerful or has more authority over the victim, because of different positions in educational, social, political and employment settings. A difference in age is also the main factor.

There are certain conditions that define harassment relationships:

• Anyone can be a perpetrator, including a parent, legal guardian, relative, teacher, client, colleague, student, a stranger or even a friend.

- Harassment can take place whether there are witnesses or not.

- The offender may not realize that their behavior is offensive and unlawful.

- Cases of harassment can occur in circumstances where the victim is not aware of what's going on.

- Harassment can have severe effects on the victim, including social withdrawal, sleep problems, stress, eating disorders and other health problems.

- The perpetrator may not be of the opposite sex.

- Harassment can happen as a result of a misunderstanding between the perpetrator and the victim.

Sexual harassment was first codified in American law following a series of harassment incidents in the 1970s and 1980s. Most women who first reported these incidents were African American. Many of them had been former civil rights activists who implemented the principles of civil rights to sex discrimination. For example, activists like Lin Farley, Susan Meyer, and Karen Sauvigne formed the Working Women's Institute which was among the first organizations publicly condemn sexual harassment in the late 1970s.

Since the early 1990s, the number of sexual harassment cases reported in the US and Canada rose by 58 percent. This rate has been increasing gradually ever since.

CHAPTER TWO:
ONLINE SEXUAL HARASSMENT

Nowadays, in a world with advanced technological developments – the internet which enables global social interactions, more incidents of sexual harassment are occurring online through social media, video games, and chat rooms.

The internet has allowed a lack of accountability to a great extent, unspecified legal boundaries, anonymous authorities, and ineffective sanctions, therein permitting harassers to act as they wish without consequential restraints.

Online interactions have become more like peer relationships, making people feel more confident to speak out and behave in an offensive manner. Online anonymity permits internet users like cyber-sexual harassers, to act in extremely negative ways that psychologically harm other internet users.

About 40 percent of people who access the internet have reported some form of harassment at some point.

These experiences range from mild forms of harassment like name-calling to more serious forms such as threats or stalking.

Online harassment is divided into two main categories: information received by a victim and information posted about a victim.

Social media is the most common platform where harassment occurs, but such incidents can also take place within the comments section of a website and through personal email.

Online sexual harassment refers to unwelcome sexual conduct on any digital platform. It is a form of sexual violence and comprises of a broad range of behaviors that involve the use of online content on diverse platforms, public or private.

This type of harassment can evoke a feeling of being threatened, humiliated, exploited, coerced, discriminated against or sexualized. It can result in embarrassment and pose a threat to one's physical safety, in the event of stalking. It mostly occurs among young people.

Sometimes, cyber-sexual harassers take advantage of the internet to connect with acquaintances from offline social environments like school or work. Strangers can also weasel their way to a victim's profile and initiate unwanted sexual attention, exploitation or coercion.

Recently, more women have reported receiving unsolicited pornographic materials stalking or harassment on the internet. Research shows that men will unconsciously misuse the power to sexually harass women. This is probably the case in online sexual harassment. Becoming sexually attracted to another internet user can motivate the harasser to use his power to sexually harass another internet user. Additionally, cyber feminists state that it is the threat to internet resources that provokes a male internet user to sexually harass female internet users. Since women have become more active on the internet, men feel threatened by women's increasing participation in a platform that has until recently been mostly dominated by men, eventually resulting in men harassing women online.

Sexist nicknames and misogynistic behavior are often more offensive online since the words are written out instead of being verbally spoken, making them have a more severe effect on the victim. Furthermore, comments regarding dressing have a more negative impact because of the level of inappropriateness resulting from the absence of face-to-face contact.

Cyberstalking

Cyberstalking comprises a group of behaviors whereby information and communication technology is used to provoke emotional distress to an individual.

It is closely associated with online sexual harassment, cyberbullying and cyber lurking since many similar techniques are used. Social media, blogs, photo sharing apps, and numerous other commonly used online sharing activities give cyberstalkers tons of information that helps them draw up their harassment plan. They gather personal data (profile pages) and make notes of frequented locations (photo tags, blog posts). The cyberstalker can then start compiling records on an individual's daily life.

Since it can be hard or impossible to find a legal resolution if the cyberstalker lives in another country, you should not give up on reporting the abuse to relevant sites and the police. The stalker could be lying about their location and reside in the same country or city as you. It's safer to take action and treat the situation as a threat to your security.

When it comes to real-life stalkers, their aim is to control the victim, and this is achieved through intimidation. In cyberspace, the stalker may feel bolder than they really are, posing behind aliases, and trusting the anonymity of the internet.

Being the victim can make you feel paralyzed and helpless, but there are ways to take control and remain safe. Many victims of cyberstalking have been involved in some form of relationship with the cyberstalker. They could be a former girlfriend or boyfriend, an estranged or ex-husband/wife, or someone you've had an intimate relationship with, that didn't work out well. They could even be a former roommate or friend. Since you had a relationship with them in the real world, they had access to your computer, mobile phone, wireless router, or other devices, hence finding an easy way to eventually stalk you.

Victims of cyberstalking should take the following steps:

- If you're a minor, inform your parents, guardian or a trusted adult.

- Present a complaint with the cyber stalker's Internet service provider

- Compile evidence, document instances and create a log of attempts to end the harassment.

- Present documents to local law enforcement and contact legal avenues.

- Create a new email address and have secure privacy settings on public sites and apps.

- Install privacy protection software.

- Ask for the removal of sensitive personal information from online directories.

Main Factors That Affect Online Sexual Harassment

Gender and vulnerability

This harassment occurs in a gendered context and is profoundly based on structural relationships of inequality between the male and female genders. It causes disproportionately negative results and encounters for women and girls. Matter of fact, girls are more likely to be targeted with online sexual harassment than boys, especially in some contexts, with these occurrences mostly leading to more negative outcomes for girls.

Discrimination

Online sexual harassment can occur simultaneously with discrimination and hate crimes, centered on an individual's actual or perceived gender, gender identity, sexual orientation, race, religion, disability or special educational need. Young people in any of these groups may experience diverse forms of online sexual harassment. The undesirable outcome is usually a more negative imprint in both the short and long term, in addition to multiple hindrances that can prevent them from getting access to the right support.

There are four main types of online sexual harassment:

Unwanted Sexualization

A person is subjected to unwanted sexual requests, comments, and content.

This includes various actions like:

• Sexualized comments, which are often posted in photos.

• Sexualized viral campaigns that manipulate or pressurize people to take part.

• Sending sexual content to someone, like photos, messages or emojis without their consent.

• Unwanted sexual advances or requests for sexual favors.

• Jokes that are sexual in nature.

• Rating an individual's attractiveness, sexual appeal or sexual activity

• Editing or altering someone's photos to make them appear sexual

Non-consensual Sharing of Explicit Images and Videos

In this type of harassment, a person's sexual images and videos are shared or taken without their consent.

This includes different actions such as:

• Sexual images or videos taken without consent, often known as 'creepshots' or upskirting.

- Sexual images or videos taken consensually but shared to third parties or the public without consent ('revenge porn')

- Non-consensual sexual acts (for example rape); recorded digitally and most likely shared.

Threats, Coercion, and Exploitation

A person receives sexual threats. They are often coerced to engage in sexual behavior online. Sometimes, a person can be blackmailed with sexual content.

This harassment occurs within a wide range of actions such as:

- Harassing or forcing someone online to share sexual images of themselves or participate in sexual behavior online or offline.

- Threatening to publish sexual content (photos, videos, rumors) to scare, coerce or blackmail someone. This is referred to as sextortion.

- Online threats of a sexual nature (for example rape threats)

- Influencing others online to participate in sexual violence.

• Inciting someone to participate in sexual behavior and then sharing its evidence in the form of videos, photos or audio recording.

Sexualized Bullying

In this case, an individual is targeted by and systematically isolated from a group or community using sexual content that embarrasses, upsets or discriminates against them. Such harassment encompasses:

• Rumors, lies or gossip about sexual behavior posted online either naming someone directly or indirectly referring to someone.

• Humiliating or discriminatory sexual language and online name-calling.

• Impersonating someone and ruining their reputation by sharing sexual content or sexually harassing others.

• Personal information posted non-consensually online to evoke sexual harassment.

• Being bullied because of real or perceived gender and/or sexual orientation.

• Body-shaming

• 'Outing' someone whereby their sexuality or gender identity is publicly revealed online without their consent.

These forms of harassment are mostly experienced at the same time and can take place simultaneously with offline encounters of sexual harassment.

Online sexual harassment has far-reaching negative effects on the victim. The person may feel scared because of threats and exploitation. They might feel that their dignity has been stained, and could end up feeling ashamed or guilty. A victim may conclude that they are to blame for their unpleasant online experience. Feelings of discrimination and sexualization are also common.

However, individuals respond differently to online sexual harassment. The effects of harassment can be visible in the short-term, but in some cases, they have long-term implications on well-being and mental health.

Long-term effects can worsen due to multiple instances of victimization, for example, if the explicit content is re-shared online, or if the initial impact of harassment resurfaces later. Witnesses of online sexual harassment can also be affected.

The occurrence of online sexual harassment among young people often takes place in a peer-to-peer context and is typically centered around local communities and schools, mostly happening online in front of an actively participating audience.

Sometimes, adults also harass young people or other adults online.

Avoiding Online Sexual Harassment

Despite the pressure to engage in unacceptable sexual conduct, young people can still avoid being a part of this harassment by taking the following steps:

• Don't give in to peer pressure. A person may be under pressure to fit in or be acknowledged in a peer group. This can force them to unwillingly engage in online sexual harassment. However, young people can stand firm in their decision to follow what's right. They can open up to parents or teachers about the pressure, wrong friendships or stereotypes, and get advice that will help them resist unacceptable behavior.

• Know the boundaries. It's easy for young people to describe online sexual harassment as a joke. They may even criticize the victim for failing to understand the joke. Such jokes can go too far and seriously hurt the victim. Therefore, the youth should build their empathy and judgment skills by participating in activities such as role-plays based on scenarios and discussions in order to understand how online sexual harassment affects the victim.

• Don't engage. It's possible to refrain from sharing or approving abusive content, an action which may further hurt the victim. Young people can use the internet for better purposes by resisting harmful behavior.

• Instead of seeking retaliation after a breakup, it's wiser to ask for help. Retaliation forces one to intimate photos or videos, some of which may be fabricated, to protect their reputation. Other peers usually join in and the result is violated privacy, explosive emotions, and embarrassment. Anyone going through a breakup needs help to deal with hurt, bitterness and pain. They should seek advice and talk about their feelings with someone they trust, instead of using the internet to let out their emotions.

• Report any incidents of online sexual harassment. A trustworthy adult can give guidelines on how to correctly report a case of harassment.

How to Deal with Online Sexual Harassment

It will be helpful to install a filtering system on your computer that automatically scans and eliminates e-mail messages from specific individuals or subject matters. This type of technology enables you to successfully prevent your computer from displaying items sent from particular people or content related to certain subjects or topics.

In case you're participating in real-time discussion forums, you can set your computer to block messages being sent by another user who you feel is harassing you, or who is using offensive language.

If you happen to be a victim of harassment, don't hesitate to report the behavior to the host of the website. Taking this bold step may result in the successful banning of the harasser from that website – they won't find a platform through which to carry out their offensive conduct.

Another effective way of warding off online harassment is protecting yourself from involuntarily having to see content that you may find offensive whenever you are searching for information online. Most computers have internet access controls that are specifically designed for parents to prevent their children from accessing inappropriate sites. You can personally use those controls for your own benefit so that you don't have to view offensive material.

It's important to always be cautious when choosing what type of information about yourself you post on the internet. Don't give online harassers a chance by showcasing your intimate details. For example, if you have you have created a personal website whereby family and friends can keep up with your hectic lifestyle, you may consider to either create a site that allows access for designated users only, or you may stop posting details of yourself on a website that anyone can access.

If you are an employer, consider installing a computer program that can carry out a cursory examination of e-mails within your system and which can identify and block e-mails that have offensive or inappropriate keywords.

An anti-spam program is another useful tool for preventing online sexual harassment. Spam refers to unsolicited online advertisements, most of which you may find inappropriate or offensive. There are genuine programs available that can read and interpret the content as spam and stop it from reaching you.

And whether you've been accused of harassment or are being harassed, your situation often has serious effects on your emotions. It would be wise to speak with a legal professional before anything spirals out of control. An employment law attorney can examine the occurrences that are causing you to worry and provide useful insight into your rights and alternatives for how to deal with your issues.

The Impact of Online Sexual Harassment

Based on a 2013 study, victims of cyberstalking reported that they were forced to take time off work, switch or quit their job or school at higher rates than victims of traditional stalking. The same study shows that the average financial impact of cyberstalking per victim is $1,200, which mostly covers legal fees, property damage, transport expenses, and the cost of getting a new phone number. On the contrary, the estimated cost of traditional stalking victims was about $500, which is more than double the amount of cyberstalking.

Threats of sexual and gender-based violence, death threats, online defamation, and disinformation campaigns – mostly of a sexualized nature, and often indicating the victim's real-life addresses — are harmful tools used to torture and scare off women who boldly speak out.

Some major events globally have proved this:

In Canada, a deadly rampage in April which left 10 people dead and wounded 14 – most of them women – was reportedly driven in part by the suspected perpetrator's radicalization through "incel" hate groups which operated online. In Iraq, many female parliamentary candidates have reportedly encountered online defamation campaigns, most of which include the sharing of faked photos and videos designed to intimidate, humiliate and discredit them.

In Italy, the speaker of Parliament, Laura Boldrini, has boldly dealt with countless death threats and threats of sexual torture. In one instance, the mayor of one town posted on Facebook that a convicted rapist should be sent to her house "to put a smile on her face". And in a platform that has been identified as GamerGate, thousands of anonymous online threats of murder and rape have been directed at women who criticized misogyny in video game culture.

The objective of these sadistic attacks is to stop women from speaking out. That's what Swedish broadcaster Alexandra Pascalidou told a European Commission panel in 2016. "They keep telling me to … kill myself or they will shoot me, cut my tongue off, break my fingers one by one. They keep threatening me with gang rapes and sexual torture."

Female politicians are usually among the worst affected in the context of tweets involving the most critical category, which is threats of sexual violence. Many female broadcasters and news presenters who have been interviewed are also at risk of dangerous exposure to significant levels of abuse in their workplaces. These women are frequently and relentlessly blasted with tweets describing their appearance and their bodies, with many abusers sliding into the unacceptable sexually explicit, hostile and threatening territory each day.

Furthermore, these attacks are shockingly common and widespread. In 2014, the EU Fundamental Rights Agency discovered that nearly a quarter of the women interviewed had encountered online harassment.

According to a 2017 Pew survey in the U. S., 14% of adults reported that they experienced online harassment specifically because of their political views. Around one-quarter of Americans (27%) stated that they decided not to post anything on social media after witnessing other people going through harassment, while more than one-in-ten (13%) say they have quit using an online service after witnessing other users participate in harassing behaviors.

The anxiety and fear experienced by the victims are worsened by a glaring possibility of physical harm, not to mention damage to daily life caused by the sharing of fake and sexually explicit images or other malicious allegations. In a recent survey of eight countries, Amnesty International observed that at least 41% of women who had been harassed online were worried about their physical safety, and 24% feared for their family's safety since online predators who attack women often direct detailed and horrific threats against their families.

Additionally, emotional turmoil and psychological distress frequently afflict victims of cyberstalking and harassment, especially because of their conviction that the perpetrator is inescapable. Due to its round-the-clock presence, cyber harassment is, in fact, more harmful to a victim's mental well-being than other types of harassment or stalking.

The violation of a victim's right to privacy, freedom of expression, and unlimited participation in economic, social, cultural and political affairs is a serious concern. Online forms of intimidation and violence may also weaken the efficiency of women's networks, which often use online platforms as their main mode of communication and mobilization. These outcomes are further complicated by the high degree of impunity enjoyed by online harassers.

If these worrying patterns continue, instead of empowering people, online platforms may end up escalating sex and gender-based discrimination and violence – creating an environment in which no one feels safe online or offline.

To solve this problem, the media should take responsibility for the manner in which they represent women in the press. It's not only the unmistakable glaring examples but a more low-level, pervasive and typical portrayal of women as objects of desire to be scrutinized and commented on — that makes it right for the society to endlessly judge women based on their appearance rather than their talents, ability or intellect. The society should support women who call out their harassers online. We shouldn't be reluctant to retweet their messages and spread messages of support with our own followers. This will enable us to emphasize that sexism online will no longer be tolerated.

CHAPTER THREE: SEXUAL HARASSMENT IN THE WORKPLACE

Harassment in the workplace comes in several forms and affects many people in different industries. At times, it happens in obvious ways, although in most cases it goes ignored, unreported, overlooked, and misunderstood. It occurs based on diverse reasons – gender, race, disability, age, ethnicity, political preferences, job status, color or religion.

A single incident is enough to be termed as sexual harassment – it doesn't have to be persistent.

Although men experience sexual harassment in the workplace, it disproportionately affects women. Women in positions of leadership are more likely to be harassed because they are in leadership, which means sexual harassment is a way of enforcing appropriate gender behavior by those who consider their supervisory power as illegitimate or easily undermined. Harassment in these cases aims to take away the authority of women in supervisory roles by equating them with lower-ranking employees.

Many industries have seen rampant sexual harassment. For example, about 41% of women in media and entertainment state that they've experienced sexual harassment from a colleague or boss at some point in their careers, according to a new report conducted by the Center for Talent Innovation (CTI). This is the highest rate among white-collar industries.

The report discovered that across eight industry categories, 34% of women and 13% of men have been victims of sexual harassment, described as an unwanted sexual advance or obscene remark. The results demonstrate that the problem is unusually widespread in the media, an industry that has recently seen sexual-misconduct claims and accusations against once-high-ranking executives.

According to a co-president in the CTI, the power dynamics in the media are more skewed than in other industries. Media is a very relationship-driven industry, where rewards in terms are of money, visibility, and influence controlled by a handful of gatekeepers. Powerful media figures have misused their power in these ways. Ultimately, observations have proved that sexual harassment is about power.

In contrast to conventional knowledge, the CTI study found that the financial services industry — a historically male-dominated industry — had the lowest reported rate of sexual harassment among women among the industries examined. The reason could be because three decades ago, banking and finance companies were faced with many class-action sex harassment lawsuits, and that seems to have resulted in a shift in corporate policies and culture.

The study reported that people who have faced sexual harassment on the job are less likely to be satisfied with their jobs (and more likely to realize advancement in their careers) than those who have been not harassed — and the same is true for workers who have been told by a co-worker about an experience of harassment or sexual assault.

Other observations from the CTI study include:

- Among women who have been harassed, 72% were harassed by someone more senior in their careers.

- 57% of men who have been harassed were harassed by other men.

- 25% percent of Baby Boomers, 24% of Generation Xers, and 23% of millennials have experienced sexual harassment from a colleague.

- Hispanic and white women are the most likely to say they have experienced sexual harassment at work (37% for both groups).

- 23% of black women who have been harassed were harassed by other women, compared with 10% of white women, 10% of Latinas, and 5% of Asian women.

Harassment programs must include the possibility that the target of harassment is of higher rank in the organization than the harasser. Sexual harassment and assault at work have serious consequences on the well-being of women and can ruin the reputation of their employers. Women who are victims of harassment may face a broad range of negative consequences, including physical and mental health issues, career interruptions, and lower salaries. In addition, sexual harassment may hinder or discourage women from venturing into better-paying jobs and may contribute to the long-term gender wage gap.

Effects of Sexual Harassment in the Workplace

Harassment mainly results in lower productivity and job dissatisfaction. This outcome is not just for people who experience it, but for those who witness it as well. Reports of harassment have a negative effect on the consumers' perception of the involved brand. Consumers who observe or suspect harassment at an organization may not consider repurchasing from the brand and often show less interest in learning about the company's new products or services.

Numerous studies have proved that perceived sexual harassment in the workplace is the main culprit for negative attitudes toward a brand and brand image. On the other hand, if internal stakeholders step up and understand, accept, and implement organizational brand values, including a dignified corporate culture, the company has a chance to reclaim a competitive advantage in the marketplace. The brand also gets an opportunity to thrive. Every entrepreneur and executive needs to know that internal brand strategies and integrity are essential for long-term business success.

Employee turnover may be a true reflection of the biggest single component of the overall expenses incurred due to sexual harassment. Harassment can lead to massive loss of finances which would be used for better purposes in a company. The fines that come with harassment should be enough reason for any organization to treat the problem seriously. The indirect costs of harassment can cripple the implementation of important policies in a company.

Studies show that sexual harassment is linked to several physical health problems like headaches, fatigue, sleep problems, nausea, and gastric problems. People who go through harassment eventually endure a wide range of psychological and physical consequences. Studies have linked harassment to a higher risk of developing depression, anxiety, PTSD, substance abuse, unintentional weight gain or loss, insomnia, drug and alcohol abuse, and cardiovascular and musculoskeletal problems. These issues are compounded by prolonged harassment.

Harassment affects victims' colleagues and co-workers as well. Employees who witness or perceive abuse in their workplace can also developmental and physical troubles.

Harassment results in a turnover. When they have to deal with incidents of harassment and a culture that allows misbehavior and incivility, employees tend to quit their jobs. Researchers admit that turnover comprises the greatest single element of the average cost of sexual harassment, which amounts to hundreds of millions of dollars per year. The reverse is also true: employers who take bold, practical steps to stop harassment manage to retain employees longer than their counterparts.

Harassment damages an organization's reputation and ability to develop new business. Alleged misconduct and incivility towards employees discourage not only current and prospective employees but current and future clients. Regardless of who the harasser is, the unpleasant effects of harassment can cause a serious downfall to a company. In fact, the reputational costs alone can have adverse consequences, specifically where it is discovered that managers ignored a well-known harasser for years.

The mere perception of sexual harassment among a workgroup can create a hostile and tense environment, negatively impacting the group's day-to-day operations. Employees are more likely to reject work and avoid each other.

Reduced productivity is a major effect of harassment. There is credible research to show that workplace sexual harassment is associated with less motivation and commitment, as well as withdrawal. This negative effect is not limited to the targets and can also have an impact on those who witness or hear about harassment. It reduces both individual and team performance. One study of 27 teams at a food services organization showed that sexual hostility—a form of sexual harassment that consists of explicitly sexual verbal and nonverbal behaviors that are insulting—is destructive for team processes and performance.

The aftermath of harassment can become a pattern that spreads throughout the workplace and crushes long-term team performance. Harassment brings down an organization's bottom line. The allegations, management and investigation processes deplete a departments' time and resources. Victims and bystanders usually report difficulty concentrating and participating in work-related activities. Employee involvement and teamwork go down while cases of tardiness and absenteeism increase.

One study observed that employees, both female and male, who witnessed hostility directed at female coworkers (both incivility and sexually harassing behavior) were more likely to develop lower psychological well-being. These declines in mental health were consequently linked to lower physical well-being. The triggers of these effects can come from empathy and worry for the victim, concern about the lack of integrity in their workplace, or fear of becoming the next victim.

Instances of workplace harassment include discrimination such as:

• Making negative comments about an employee's personal religious beliefs, or attempting to convert them to a certain religious ideology

• Using racist slang, phrases, or nicknames

- Making remarks about an individual's skin color or other ethnic traits

- Displaying racist drawings, or posters that could be offensive to a particular group

- Making offensive gestures

- Making offensive reference to an individual's mental or physical disability

- Sharing inappropriate images, videos, emails, letters, or notes

- Offensively talking about negative racial, ethnic, or religious stereotypes

- Making derogatory age-related comments

- Wearing clothes that could be offensive to a particular ethnic group.

During an interview, it's not advisable for employers to ask about your race, gender, religion, marital status, age, disabilities, ethnic background, country of origin, sexual preferences, or age. If this occurs, it should serve as a red flag that you may not want to continue with your candidacy with this employer.

How to Deal with Workplace Sexual Harassment

All occurrences of sexual harassment – no matter how big or small or who is involved – require employers, managers or employees to act quickly and appropriately.

Whichever your position may be in a company, here's how you can respond to sexual harassment:

If someone approaches you with unwanted sexually-driven intentions, learn to clearly say no. Inform the person that their behavior is offensive to you. Stand your ground and decline all invitations. If the harasser continues, ask them to stop and put it in writing. Ensure you keep a copy of this written communication.

Write down a description of what happened. As soon as you experience sexual harassment, note down the dates, times, places, and any witnesses who saw what happened. If you're comfortable, request your co-workers to write down what they saw or heard. You might discover that they have ever experienced the same thing at some point.

It's true that others may and possibly will read this written record as time goes by. It's therefore good to store them in a safe place. However, don't keep the record at work. This could be risky if the harasser is still lurking around.

Keep a paper trail. When it's time to report the incident to your employer, present it in writing. Give details of the problem and how you'd like it to be solved. This compiles a written record of when you complained and what followed afterward. Remember to store copies of everything you send and receive from your employer.

With your records ready, take action and report the harassment. You might consider informing your supervisor, your human resources department or another department or executive within your organization who has the authority to stop the harassment. It's advisable to write down your complaint.

Learn more about your employer's grievance and complaint procedures. Many employers have policies and procedures that describe how to file and respond to sexual harassment complaints. To understand your employer's policies, request and read through a copy of your employee manual, any written personnel policies, and consult an official in the human resources department. These procedures may be helpful in stopping the harassment and resolving the issue. In the long run, following your employer's complaint procedures (if any are provided) will prove that you did your best to bring the harassment to your employer's attention.

Consider the help of your union. If you belong to a union, it would be better to file a formal grievance through the union and try to get a union official to assist you to get through the grievance process. Get a copy of your collective bargaining agreement to confirm if it highlights the difficulties you are experiencing. Remember that if you use your union's grievance procedure, you must still file a complaint or charge of discrimination with a government agency before presenting a lawsuit in federal or state court.

Visit a government agency to file a discrimination complaint. If you wish to file a lawsuit in federal or state court, you must first file a formal sexual harassment complaint or charge with the federal Equal Employment Opportunity Commission.

And lastly, file a lawsuit. After filing a formal complaint with the EEOC and/or your state's fair employment agency, the next step is filing a lawsuit. The resolutions or relief you can seek in a lawsuit will be broad, but they might include money damages, going back to your job (if you've been fired or transferred to another position), and/or convincing your employer reform company practices to prevent future sexual harassment from taking place. If you are seriously considering filing a lawsuit, you should contact a lawyer to help you with the process.

According to federal law, you have a period of 300 days from an experience of sexual harassment to file a complaint with the EEOC. Under your state's fair employment law, if there's one in your state, you may have as little as 180 days to file a complaint. Filing deadlines differ from state to state so it is good to check with the EEOC or a legal organization to learn about the time limits. Contact Equal Rights Advocates or a lawyer to know what you need to do and, the duration required.

How to Develop a Strategy for Ending Sexual Harassment

Every employee needs a working environment that's not stained with unlawful harassment. A harassment prevention strategy enables organizations to articulate their opinions on harassment in the workplace and draw up the steps they will take to ensure all employees are held responsible for acting in line with these opinions.

Business owners and company executives should adopt leadership and practice commitment to an inclusive, diverse and respectful workplace in which harassment will not thrive. These principles must come from the leadership of every organization.

In every level across all positions, an organization should have systems in place that hold employees responsible for meeting all requirements and expectations.

Leaders can take these steps to create a holistic harassment prevention initiative:

Leadership and Accountability

The most important strategy in creating an effective harassment prevention initiative is for the leadership of an organization to solidify a culture of dignity and respect in which harassment is not permitted.

Firm Policies

An organization needs to map out a comprehensive policy against harassment that highlights the behaviors that will not be tolerated in the workplace and the procedures to abide by in reporting and responding to any incident of harassment.

Compliance Training

An all-round strategy provides training to employees whereby they learn about an employer's policy, reporting systems, and investigations. Managers should also learn how to handle harassment incidents properly and effectively before they unfavorably advance to legal issues.

Reporting and Investigation

Every administration should provide reporting systems for allegations of harassment for both employees who have encountered harassment as well as those who have witnessed incidents of harassment. Throughout the reporting and investigation process, the laid out strategies should be strictly followed and the right disciplinary steps are taken to deal with perpetrators of sexual harassment, regardless of their position in the organization.

A firm can maintain consistency in ending sexual harassment by:

- Reviewing strategies and policies to ensure they are up-to-date and accessible to everyone who needs them.

- Constantly encouraging reporting in the workplace, for example by recognizing the effort of managers and giving them credit for taking steps to encourage reporting and promoting appropriate behavior.

- Clarifying the right standards of behavior through discussion, leadership, and modeling. This gives everyone in the company a clear picture of the way they're expected to conduct themselves at all times, even during company events.

- Forming staff contact officers who can give confidential information about employees' rights and complaints procedures. These officers will provide much-needed support when an employee has to deal with sexual harassment.

When companies recognize work-related factors related to increased risk of sexual harassment and assault in the workplace, they can develop ways to eliminate sexual harassment in specific occupations and situations. Some major risk factors include:

• Working for tips. Workers in industries like accommodation and food services—which employ wait staff and hotel housekeepers who are usually categorized as "tipped"— makeup 14 percent of harassment charges to the EEOC, which is significantly higher than the sector's share of total employment. A survey by the Restaurant Opportunities Center observes that women who work in restaurants depend on tips for their main source of income in states where the sub-minimum wage is $2.13. These women are twice as likely to face sexual harassment from managers, co-workers, and customers. The survey also showed that many women employees keep on working in tipped jobs in spite of harassment because tips are a valued part of their income.

• Lack of legal immigration status or having a temporary work visa. Undocumented workers or those on temporary work visas are mostly at a higher risk of harassment and assault. Agriculture, food processing and garment factories, as well as domestic work and janitorial services, are sectors where many undocumented and immigrant women work. The victims of sexual violence at work who file charges have the same protection against deportation as survivors of domestic violence through U-visas. Still, many believe that reporting harassment or assault will put their immigration status at risk. Others may not be aware of their rights or may find it difficult to access legal support since some of them are not fluent in English. In addition, retaliation against women who speak up against sexual assault in the workplace may precipitate threats to alert Immigration and Customs Enforcement or to revoke temporary work visas.

• Working in an isolated field. Many workers, for example, female janitors, domestic care workers, agricultural workers, and hotel workers who often work in isolated contexts report higher than average incidents of sexual harassment and assault. Isolation makes women vulnerable to abusers who may feel confident because the situation is worsened by a lack of witnesses.

In 2015, Frontline reported that ABM (regarded as the largest employer of janitors) was faced with 42 lawsuits brought against it in the previous two decades for allegations of workplace sexual harassment, assault, or rape. A National Domestic Workers Alliance and University of Chicago report discovered that 36 percent of live-in workers interviewed admitted to having been harassed, threatened, insulted or verbally abused in the previous 12 months.

• Working in an environment with significant power differentials and "rainmakers." Many workplaces have huge power differences between colleagues. These power disparities which create disparities, especially considering women's lower likelihood of holding the senior positions, are risk factors that can spark sexual harassment and assault. Workers in more junior positions may be especially worried about retaliation, the response to internal complaints, and the unchanging state of vulnerability within their job. Rainmakers such as a prominent professor, distinguished or high-earning partner, or renowned researcher may think they do not need to comply with the policies that govern other employees and may not be confronted if accused of sexual harassment or assault.

- Working in a male-dominated field. Women who work in occupations where they are a small minority, specifically in very physical settings or environments focused on traditionally male-oriented tasks may also be highly vulnerable to harassment and assault. In a survey conducted in the early 1990s, about six in ten women working in construction reported being touched or asked for sex. In another study from 2013, three in ten women construction workers reported facing sexual harassment daily or frequently, with similar numbers reporting harassment centered on sexual orientation, race, or age. A 2014 RAND study of sexual assault and harassment in the military concluded that 26 percent of active-duty women had experienced sexual harassment or gender discrimination in the past year, including almost five percent who had encountered one or more sexual assaults (compared with seven and one percent of active-duty men, respectively, according to National Defense

Research Institute 2014). A recent National Academy of Sciences study revealed high levels of harassment of women faculty and staff in academia in science, engineering, and medicine, with women in academic medicine reporting more constant gender harassment than their female counterparts in science and engineering.

These structural risk factors often go hand-in-hand and are heightened by racism, discrimination, and harassment based on age, disability, or national origin. Furthermore, working in low-wage jobs itself can accelerate a higher risk of harassment. Low-wage occupations are more likely to be available in smaller, less formalized workplaces without official complaint mechanisms. Earning low wages may also make it more hard or impossible for a worker to leave a job, or to risk losing it by filing a complaint.

Business leaders and executives should work on providing resources and training and the development of new tools. This will help prevent and address workplace sexual harassment and assault, an action that is essential to making workplaces safer and favorable for all workers and focus on sustaining productivity gains.

Labor unions should also make sure that their own policies and reporting systems align with the same standards as employer systems.

For even better outcomes, researchers should review the impact of workplace pieces of training on reducing the rate of sexual harassment in the workplace.

The federal government should carry out additional research, including developing and conducting new polls and/or adding questions to current surveys on sexual harassment and assault, through various agencies.

Employees must also take on an active role in the prevention of sexual harassment. Employees should commit to doing the following:

• Obtain and properly understand the organization's rules and policy on sexual harassment;

• Assess one's feelings, attitudes, and behaviors in relation to sexual harassment and ensure that behavior is in sync with the expectations and behavioral requirements of the organization's sexual harassment policy.

- Observe and be conscious of involving oneself in potential sexual-harassment behaviors or incidents at the workplace.

- Be sensitive to co-workers who may be offended by the verbal and non-verbal behavior of others.

- Be knowledgeable about subtle forms of sexual harassment.

- Look out for and discourage sexual actions that negatively affect work.

- Examine and pay attention to the reactions of others so as to avoid unintentional offense.

- Never assume that employees or co-workers enjoy or want to hear risqué jokes or sexually-driven comments about their appearance, or be touched, stared at, flirted with, or requested for dates or sexual favors.

- Ask yourself if your verbal or non-verbal behaviors might have a harmful impact on other co-workers' attitudes towards work.

- Scrutinize your behaviors, gestures, and comments. Ask yourself, "Could I unintentionally or unknowingly be provoking sexual interplay by the way I interact or speak?"

- Don't take sexual harassment lightly. If you think you are being sexually harassed by an individual or a group, do not dismiss it as a joke. Do not encourage the harasser by smiling, laughing at his/her jokes, or flirting back. Inform the harasser that you do not enjoy and don't like this type of attention.

- If you can, confront the sexual harasser immediately. Let them know that you find that type of attention offensive.

- If possible, tell the harasser that the behavior affects you negatively and has the capacity to negatively affecting your job.

- If you know someone who is experiencing harassment, give him or her your support. Encourage them to talk about it and to take immediate action to file a charge against the perpetrator.

- If you happen to see or hear an incident of sexual harassment or are subjected to an offensive environment, you can also take the recommended steps to resolve the harassment or co-file with the complainant.

- When a victim files a complaint, if possible, support them throughout the complaint process.

A firm's policies and innovations can have an implication on the commonly accepted or desirable behaviors or opinions expected from employees. This can be achieved through policy, or implicitly, through organizational changes that affect behavior and in turn norms.

Companies should also recognize the importance of an integrated approach since a written policy on its own is insufficient. A policy that is not implemented through communication, education, and enforcement will be of little or no impact. There is also a need for practical high-level management and modeling, including the creation and communication of policies relevant to sexual harassment as well as to gender equality in a broader perspective, and the allocation of substantial and appropriate resources for policy and training in order to ensure success. Training should also address gender-relevant cultural issues.

A positive organizational change can occur in the wider context of promoting gender equity. This has a significant impact on the scope of work within workplaces because it entails other organizational functions about sexual harassment such as workplace employment Practices, remuneration, workplace flexibility, promotion channels and many others. It's also proven that primary prevention of violence against women programming can be incorporated into a workplace setting.

Other key features that organizations should adopt are:

Organizational approaches:

• Comprehensiveness or a holistic approach: Leveraging multiple strategies formulated to promote change at multiple levels within an organization (e.g. individual, colleagues, and management), and for multiple outcomes (e.g. staff knowledge and attitudes, formal policy and practices, as well as informal culture and behaviors)

• Addressing structural factors: Dealing with structural and underlying causes of social problems for a change instead of only focusing on individual behavior or the signs of bigger problems

- Contextualized programming: devising intervention strategies that are in alignment with the broader social, economic and political context of the workplace/organization;

- Health and strengths promotion: working together to enhance current workplace/organizational resources and strengths while confronting risk factors.

- Staff engagement: partnering with workplace/organizational members in the objective of identifying targets for change and creating change strategies.

- Theory-based: grounding strategy design in a realistic theoretical rationale.

Creating a proper corporate culture is the most fundamental strategy for ending sexual harassment and assault. A stand-alone sexual harassment and assault policy should be designed separately from the normal workplace employee conduct. This is because harassment and assault are sensitive issues to address.

Employers should implement bystander training and form a dedicated group to speak confidentially in support of anyone who faces sexual harassment.

In a nutshell, an effective model for combating sexual harassment integrates:

- Raising awareness through efficient communication across organizations, highlighting the extent and nature of the harassment and how to support workers who may be experiencing it.

- Active leaders who speak out against harassment.

- Support and referral information for potential victims.

- Managers and staff who are trained to recognize the signs of harassment and respond appropriately.

- Staff who are trained to take pro-social action as bystanders when they witness harassment, sexism or discriminatory behaviors.

- Employee Codes of Conduct or Values Statements dedicated to zero-tolerance harassment, sexism, and discrimination.

- Leaders who are active in promoting gender equality, equal rights opportunities and rewards across the firm, including women's equal participation in workplace practice and decision-making.

- Encouraging and promoting women to leadership positions.
- Consistency in following a good corporate culture.
- Reviewing hiring and promotion policies to encourage equality and retention of high-ranking women employees.

Leadership commitment is another significant factor that helps reduce harassment. Accountability and engagement should be the top values they adopt. A competent leadership style creates a safe and favorable workplace setting. Leaders can influence the behavior of other employees indirectly, with the way they implement strategies. This influence can be either positive or negative.

When male leaders are involved in positive change and become accountable, they can create a bigger platform for engaging in dialogue and sharing a common commitment to improve gender equality in workplaces and more importantly, end sexual harassment.

CHAPTER FOUR:
REAL-LIFE STORIES OF SEXUAL
HARASSMENT/ASSAULT

In recent times, there have been true stories reported in the media – experiences of prominent people who at one point in their lives went through sexual harassment or assault. Their experiences vary in terms of the situations they were in when it happened, but they all illustrate the nature and extent of harassment. The aim of telling these stories is to encourage someone who has gone through the same experience and let them know they can seek support, and they are not alone.

LUCY HALE

Months after alluding to a sexual assault incident, Lucy Hale spoke up about her experience in the #MeToo era, in a cover story for Haute Living Los Angeles. "I've experienced stuff on the small side, but assault is assault. I think there are a lot of people who have been intoxicated and taken advantage of. It's happened to me and people I know. It's very common," she said. "Luckily, I've been unscathed; nothing's hurt me too badly." In January 2018, the actress referenced sexual assault in now-deleted posts on both her Twitter and Instagram pages, writing, "I never understood sexual assault until tonight. I always sympathized, but I never felt the pain of it until right now. My dignity and pride were broken. I am completely at a loss of words."

TIFFANY HADDISH

The 38year-old actress appeared on the cover of Glamour where she recounted being allegedly raped by a police cadet when she was only 17. Haddish said the incident led to her seeking help and shaped the way she approached men in her life. "That whole experience put me in such a messed-up place for a long time, and I ended up going to counseling," she said. The experience compelled her to want to make a change and help victims of sexual assault, and she's working on figuring out what actions she can take to make a difference. "I need a plan," Haddish said. "I could be a voice, but what's a voice going to do—just keep talking? Or is there action behind it?"

HALLE BERRY

The Oscar winner has previously opened up about being physically abused by a former boyfriend, telling PEOPLE in 1996 that she had been hit so hard her eardrum was punctured. "I have an understanding, a knowing. I feel like I have something that I can impart to these women," the actress revealed during a 2015 event benefitting the Jenesse Center, a national domestic violence prevention and intervention organization. "It seems like I've overcome it, but I really haven't. In the quiet of my mind, I still struggle. So while I'm helping these women, I'm helping myself through it, too."

JANE FONDA

In an interview with Brie Larson for The EDIT, the Grace and Frankie star opened up about the "extent to which a patriarchy takes a toll on females" and revealed for the first time that she was once raped. "I've been raped, I've been sexually abused as a child and I've been fired because I wouldn't sleep with my boss," she said. "I always thought it was my fault; that I didn't do or say the right thing." Fonda's difficult past, she shared, is what led her to be a passionate activist for women's rights. In 2001, the actress founded the Jane Fonda Center for Adolescent Reproductive Health, which aims to help prevent teen pregnancy. Through her work, Fonda said she wants to help abuse victims "realize that [rape and abuse is] not our fault. We were violated and it's not right."

ABIGAIL BRESLIN

Two weeks after Breslin spoke up about her own sexual assault in honor of Sexual Assault Awareness Month, the actress went on her Instagram to explain why she didn't come forward with the incident right away. "I did not report my rape. I didn't report it because of many reasons," she wrote. "I was in a relationship with my rapist and feared not being believed ... I also feared that if my case didn't lead anywhere, he would still find out and hurt me even more." The Dirty Dancing reboot star said that claims that unreported rapes "don't matter" is "unfair, untrue and unhelpful." "It's like [saying] you got a black eye from being punched in the face, but because you didn't call the police, you didn't really get a black eye," she explained, concluding: "Unreported rapes count. Reported rapes count. End of the story."

EVAN RACHEL WOOD

After her interview with Rolling Stone, the Westworld star decided to go into detail about her experience with "physical, psychological [and] sexual" abuse in an email to the magazine. "The first time I was unsure that if it was done by a partner it was still in fact rape, until too late," she wrote, revealing she was sexually assaulted twice. "Also who would believe me. And the second time, I thought it was my fault and that I should have fought back more, but I was scared," she continued. "This was many, many years ago and I, of course, know now neither one was my fault and neither one was OK." Wood explained her reasoning behind her admission: "I don't believe we live in a time where people can stay silent any longer. Not given the state our world is in with its blatant bigotry and sexism."

ASIA ARGENTO

In a New Yorker article published in October 2017, the Italian actress claimed that Hollywood producer Harvey Weinstein sexually assaulted her in 1997, forcibly performing oral sex on her. She alleges that she was invited to what was supposed to be a Miramax party at a hotel in France, but arrived to find Weinstein alone in his hotel room. "He asks me to give a massage. I was, like, 'Look man, I am no fool,' " Argento told writer Ronan Farrow of her experience. "But, looking back, I am a fool. And I am still trying to come to grips with what happened." She later added: "It wouldn't stop. It was a nightmare." Argento is among a group of women, which also includes Gwyneth Paltrow, Angelina Jolie, Cara Delevingne and Kate Beckinsale — who've accused Weinstein of sexual harassment and assault.

ALY RAISMAN

The three-time Olympic gold medalist is adding her name to the list of women who have accused former USA Gymnastics team doctor Larry Nassar of sexual abuse. The 23-year-old athlete spoke out about the alleged abuse she received at Nassar's hands in an interview with 60 Minutes. "I am angry. I'm really upset because it's been... I care a lot, you know?" Raisman revealed to the CBS News program. "I see these young girls that come up to me, and they ask for pictures or autographs, whatever it is, I just... I can't. Every time I look at them, every time I see them smiling, I just think — I just want to create change so that they never, ever have to go through this."

COREY FELDMAN

"I was [sexually] abused as a result of it, and I still deal with these issues," Feldman told PEOPLE of childhood fame. "It has been a very rough road for me." However, the actor puts on a brave face for his 12-year-old son, Zen. "I have to be a positive influence on him, and I've got to stay strong for him," he continued, referencing the hateful comments he received following his recent Today performance. "No matter how mean and awful people can be, I can't let that affect me."

In addition to these shocking yet inspiring stories, other stars have been charged with sexual assault or harassment:

BILL COSBY

Bill Cosby is a comedy legend who has entertained America and the world for decades with sitcoms "The Bill Cosby Show" and, more recently, "Kids Say the Darndest Things." Still, throughout his career, Cosby has been accused of various acts of sexual assault that have included drugging women without their knowledge or consent.

One of many accusations over a 20 year period came from Barbara Bowman who alleged Cosby sexually attacked her when she was a young actress in the late 1980s. In 2004, Andrea Constant filed a civil lawsuit against Cosby with similar accusations. The suit included 13 other alleged victims. He settled this suit out of court in 2006 for an undisclosed amount.

R KELLY

In a situation where there are many cases of allegations of sexual assault, it is difficult to compile the appropriate evidence. However, in R. Kelly's case, there was enough video content to suggest he did engage in sexual relations with at least one underage girl.

In 2008, Kelly was acquitted of all charges of possession of lewd material featuring a child and sexual acts with a child. Both Kelly and the alleged 13-year old girl denied they were the ones in the video that was mailed to The Chicago Times.

The court determined neither he nor the woman was on the tape and Kelly was released from all charges.

MYSTIKAL

Mystikal, an R&B singer, was charged with both sexual assault and extortion in 2002. The charges were based on a video confiscated by authorities that showed the alleged sexual assault.

The video apparently showed Mystikal and two other men verbally harass an adult hairstylist and force her to engage in sexual acts with them. It was also alleged that

Mystikal further sexually attacked the woman while the camera was turned off.

When a celebrity is involved in a case of sexual harassment, many issues are magnified and the already tricky legal territory can become treacherous. Not every case of celebrity sexual assault described here has led to guilty pleas, prosecution, or even sentencing. Some defenders have been acquitted of their charges, while others are still under investigation. Some cases do not involve legal charges but greatly influence public perceptions.

The Weinstein scandal sparked a national debate about sexual misconduct and mobilized many victims to come forward with accusations ranging from groping to rape against others, including former Gossip Girl actor Ed Westwick, actor Morgan Freeman, and former President George H. W. Bush. Since the New York Times and The New Yorker first published allegations of sexual harassment and rape against Harvey Weinstein by Rose McGowan, Gwyneth Paltrow, Ashley Judd and dozens of others, the troubled producer has been fired from his company. In May, Weinstein was arrested in New York on charges of rape, criminal sex act, sex abuse and sexual misconduct related to interactions with two women.

Since April 2017, many powerful people like celebrities, politicians, and CEOs, have been accused of sexual harassment, assault, or other misconduct allegations. More survivors are coming forward almost every day, many of them inspired and emboldened by those who have spoken out before.

Bloomberg reported that five women came forward to accuse the Uber investor Shervin Pishevar of sexual assault or harassment. The women told Bloomberg that Pishevar took advantage of their professional connections by using mentorship, an investment or a potential job to make unwanted advances.

In a statement to Bloomberg, representatives for Pishevar said, "We are confident that these anecdotes will be shown to be untrue." He did not immediately respond to TIME's request for comment. In November, Forbes reported that Pishevar was arrested — but never charged — in London in May for alleged rape. A spokesperson told Bloomberg: "In May 2017, Mr. Pishevar was detained briefly in London in connection with an alleged sexual assault, an allegation he categorically denied. He fully cooperated with the police investigation which was exhaustive and detailed. In July he was informed that no further action would be taken against him, and he was 'de-arrested' (a British legal term)."

NBC announced on Nov. 29 that it had fired Matt Lauer, who has co-anchored the Today show since 1997 after it received a detailed complaint about "inappropriate sexual behavior in the workplace." In a memo sent to NBC employees, NBC News Chairman Andrew Lack said: "While it is the first complaint about his behavior in the over 20 years he's been at NBC News, we were also presented with reason to believe this may not have been an isolated incident." NBC did not disclose specifics about the allegations.

Lauer said in a statement on Nov. 30: "There are no words to express my sorrow and regret the pain I have caused others by words and actions. To the people I have hurt, I am truly sorry. As I am writing this, I realize the depth of the damage and disappointment I have left behind at home and at NBC. Some of what is being said about me are untrue or mischaracterized, but there is enough truth in these stories to make me feel embarrassed and ashamed. I regret that my shame is now shared by the people I cherish dearly. Repairing the damage will take a lot of time and soul searching and I'm committed to begin that effort. It is now my full-time job. The last two days have forced me to take a very hard look at my own troubling flaws. It's been humbling. I am blessed to be surrounded by people I love. I thank them for their patience and grace."

Author Anna Graham Hunter wrote an essay for the Hollywood Reporter, in which she claims that Dustin Hoffman sexually harassed her on the set of the 1985 film Death of a Salesman when she was just 17 years old. Hunter claims that Hoffman groped her and made inappropriate comments to her.

In a statement to the Hollywood Reporter, Hoffman said: "I have the utmost respect for women and feel terrible that anything I might have done could have put her in an uncomfortable situation. I am sorry. It is not reflective of who I am." A spokesperson for Hoffman did not immediately respond to TIME's request for comment. About four other women — three who came forward on-the-record — later made allegations of sexual misconduct in stories published by Variety and The Hollywood Reporter. Hoffman's attorney told Variety that the allegations were "defamatory falsehoods."

Next, Variety reported that CBS TV Studios opened two human resources investigations into allegations of sexual harassment and discrimination against Brad Kern, the showrunner of NCIS: New Orleans, in 2016. The allegations included making sexualized remarks about women, giving women massages without their consent and mocking a nursing mother in front of her colleagues.

Variety reported that CBS found that Kern had made "insensitive" and "offensive" comments, but found no evidence of discrimination, harassment or gender bias. CBS told Variety in a statement: "We were aware of these allegations when they took place in 2016 and took them very seriously. Both complaints were acted upon immediately with investigations and subsequent disciplinary action. While we were not able to corroborate all of the allegations, we took this action to address behavior and management style, and have received no further complaints since this was implemented."

Kern, who was also the executive producer on Charmed, declined to comment to Variety. His agent did not immediately respond to TIME's request for comment.

In another incident, MMA fighter Conor McGregor happened to be under investigation in Ireland after a woman accused him of sexual assault in December, the New York Times reported on March 26. According to the Times, the woman said the alleged incident occurred at the Beacon Hotel in Dublin. McGregor has not been charged with a crime as of March 27. The news of the investigation came on the same day after McGregor announced his retirement on Twitter. McGregor has not publicly commented on the allegations, but his publicist released a statement calling his retirement unrelated to reports about the investigation.

The Las Vegas police department reopened an investigation on Oct. 1 into whether soccer player Cristiano Ronaldo sexually assaulted Kathryn Mayorga in a hotel room in 2009. Mayorga's attorney filed a civil complaint regarding her allegation last month, which also alleges that she signed a non-disclosure agreement in 2010 for an out-of-court settlement of $375,000. In a statement posted on Twitter, Ronaldo denied Mayorga's allegation. "I firmly deny the accusations being issued against me. Rape is an abominable crime that goes against everything that I am and believe in. Keen as I may be to clear my name, I refuse to feed the media spectacle created by people seeking to promote themselves at my expense," he wrote.

CHAPTER FIVE: CAUSES OF SEXUAL HARASSMENT

The causes of sexual harassment vary according to situations and individuals. Sometimes, sexual harassment becomes a tool to intimidate, disempower, and discourage women in traditionally male-dominated professions. For women in fields like the military, technology or politics men often perform such unacceptable behavior in an attempt to protect their occupational territory. Many times, the behavior goes so unchecked and unpunished by leaders of an organization that it eventually becomes a workplace norm.

With a work culture that constantly ignores such inappropriate behavior, women are often fearful about speaking out because of possible repercussions. Victims have no alternative but to keep quiet out of fear of losing their jobs or putting their careers on the line.

In many cases, sexual desire is relatively insignificant. Instead, power motives, personalities, and aggression play a bigger role. Matter of fact, sexual desire may be completely inexistent, in spite of the sexual element, when sex is used only for the purposes of humiliation and abuse. Similarly, while being male is a major risk factor for perpetration of sexual harassment, most men do not harass or abuse people.

Relationships among gender, power dynamics, and insecurity are the main factors that can precipitate harassment. In many real-world settings, it has been continuously evident that fears of incompetence lead to abuse of subordinates, probably in order to reclaim social status and alleviate negative, extremely unpleasant, and even unacceptable self-perceptions. This finding is also based on a study in which authors hypothesized that insecure men in powerful positions would be more likely to engage in sexually harassing actions.

Particularly when in a position of power, sexually aggressive men are more likely to approach female co-workers. Those same men are often inclined to interpret a woman's behavior as sexual when it isn't, an effect which is magnified when female co-workers are single or seem to be romantically available.

Men are also more likely to harass women who hold positions in the hierarchy, in an effort to re-assert higher status through domination. For example, when men believe female competitors have performed better than them on a knowledge test of stereotypically male areas of interest, during a mock job interview, those men are more likely to be sexually aggressive with female job applicants.

Personality related factors contribute to sexual harassment. A very visible factor is narcissism. More narcissistic men have been shown in research studies to be more likely to sexually harass women. Although this may be associated with a lack of empathy and feelings of entitlement, it may also be because narcissistic people embrace the hidden, embarrassing suspicion that they are not as good as others. Feeling incompetent, or believing others see them as incompetent, may push narcissistic people to try to compensate by harassing others to make themselves feel superior — even if this is a short-lived emotional fix, which often ends an escalating pattern of repeat perpetration. In addition to making up for their negative feelings, harassers may also be trying to coerce others into silence to avoid being exposed as incompetent to maintain status, (ironically increasing fears of exposure and fueling feelings of inferiority).

For men exclusively, being in power and fearing that others see oneself as incompetent and inferior uniquely merge to precipitate sexual harassment of female subordinates. This effect has been proved to extend to subordinate males, and is more evident with ethnic minorities, people who are gay/queer, and those with disabilities).When a man in power is not able to deal with feelings of insecurity in his own eyes and the eyes of others — and he is presented with a chance to harass against a woman in a subordinate position, when he believes he can do so without being apprehended — the conditions exist for sexual harassment to increase, because that man can discharge unacceptable feelings while restoring a fragile identity of strength by doing so.

The risk is accelerated by narcissistic personality traits and possibly the existence of a current need for sexual gratification — through sexuality itself may have no role in contributing to sexual harassment. Furthermore, individual, cultural, and systemic factors that encourage silence and the mistreatment of subjugated groups make it easy for some people to commit crimes without being confronted or apprehended.

Lower self-efficacy also presents greater chances of sexually harassing others. Women are significantly less likely to harass male subordinates than men are to harass female subordinates. For men only, escalating fears of negative evaluation from others increases the chances they will sexually harass female subordinates. Fears of negative evaluation from others predict higher chances of sexual harassment only for men in a position of power, even after considering the effects of narcissism and self-efficacy.

Approval of sexual objectification is another cause of harassment. Many men have been raised in a culture that reduces women to sexualized objects, which makes them treat female colleagues in a less than professional manner. Women in certain jobs, specifically those in which physical appearance plays a role, sometimes experience increased levels of sexual harassment because their jobs implicitly permit their sexual objectification. Some men perceive this as the ticket to process and react to these women as fantasy sex objects without personal sexual boundaries.

Sexually violent men are considered to differ from other men when it comes to impulsivity and antisocial tendencies. They also tend to have an exaggerated or overly high sense of masculinity. Additionally, sexual violence is associated with a preference for impersonal sexual relationships rather than emotional bonding, characterized by having many sexual partners and the inclination to fulfill personal interests at the expense of others. Another adverse association involves hostile attitudes on gender, with perceptions that assert women are opponents to be challenged and conquered.

Childhood environments that are physically violent, emotionally unsupportive and are associated with competition for meager resources have been linked to sexual violence. Sexually aggressive behavior in young men, for instance, has been influenced by witnessing family violence and having emotionally distant and uncaring fathers. Men who come from families with strongly patriarchal structures are also more likely to become violent, to rape and use sexual coercion against women, in addition to abusing their intimate partners, than men brought up in homes that are more egalitarian.

Drug-facilitated sexual assault (DFSA), also referred to as predator rape, is a sexual assault conducted after the victim has become incapacitated due to having consumed alcoholic drinks or other drugs. Alcohol has been proved to play a big role in certain types of sexual assault, as have some other drugs, especially cocaine. Alcohol has a psychopharmacological effect of reducing inhibitions, impairing judgments and weakening the ability to interpret cues. Nevertheless, the biological links between alcohol and violence are complex. Research on the social anthropology of alcohol consumption indicates that connections between violence, drinking, and drunkenness are learned socially rather than in a universal way.

Some researchers have observed that alcohol may act as cultural break time, offering the opportunity for antisocial behavior. Therefore, people are more likely to act violently when drunk because they don't immediately realize that they will be held accountable for their actions. Some forms of group sexual violence are also associated with drinking. In these settings, taking alcohol is an act of group bonding, where inhibition collectively decreases and individual judgment ceded in favor of the group.

Another factor involving social relationships is a family's response that blames women without punishing men, focusing instead on restoring the lost family honor. Such a response creates an environment in which rape or assault can take place with impunity.

Factors operating at a societal level that can cause sexual violence include laws and national policies generally relating to gender equality and to sexual violence more specifically, including norms regarding the use of violence. Although the various factors operate largely at a local level, within families, schools, workplaces, and communities, there are also influences from the laws and norms operating at a national and even global level.

Social norms also play a role. Sexual violence committed by men is to a large extent linked to ideologies of male sexual entitlement. These belief systems offer women extremely few legitimate options to decline sexual advances. Some men therefore simply ignore the possibility that their sexual advances towards a woman might be declined or that a woman has the right to make an autonomous decision about engaging in sexual activity.

Societal norms around the use of violence as a means to accomplish objectives have been strongly connected with the prevalence of rape. In societies where the ideology of male superiority is strong, depicting dominance, physical strength, and male honor, rape is more common. Countries with a culture of violence, or where violent conflict occurs, experience an increase in nearly all forms of violence, including sexual violence.

CHAPTER SIX:
SEXUAL HARASSMENT IN
ACADEMIC INSTITUTIONS

Statistics show that female students who are enrolled in traditionally male-dominated fields are more likely to experience sexual harassment and assault. A recent study of the University of Texas system discovered that 1 in 5 female science students, 1 in 4 female engineering students and nearly 1 in 2 female medical students reported encountering sexual harassment at high rates.

Graduate students are not excluded from facing sexual harassment and assault. Higher Ed Jobs stated that more than 1 in 3 female graduate students and nearly 1 in 4 male graduate students reported experiences of sexual harassment. More than half of the cases involved professors who were involved in multiple cases of sexual harassment.

Most cases given much attention by the media involve a professor, coach or adviser as the perpetrator of sexual misconduct, but the surprising fact is that they can also be the victims.

Faculty and non-faculty staff members are not immune to sexual harassment, abuse of power and sexual coercion. One study observing the effects of sexual harassment found that 58 percent of female faculty and non-faculty staff had experienced sexual harassment.

Similar to any other work environment, universities and colleges may have power differentials and hierarchies that put employees in a vulnerable state. Victims of harassment in any institution experience high levels of stress decreased productivity and low job satisfaction.

Examples of situations involving harassment include:

• A professor makes multiple unwanted advances toward the school librarian.

• A departmental chair offers a professor tenure in exchange for sexual relations.

• A dean sends several inappropriate sexual emails to a professor

There are high costs that result from sexual misconduct. The negative effects of sexual harassment reach farther beyond the victim's experiences. The affected institution often pays a huge financial and reputational price, especially if they fail to respond and properly handle the complaint.

The Wall Street Journal reported that "in 2016 and 2017 alone, 22 public universities and systems paid more than $10.5 million across 59 settlements involving sexual harassment claims made by students, faculty, and staff". The majority of settlements were centered on the schools' mishandling of claims.

The largest settlement, for nearly $2.5 million, involved a 2016 lawsuit against the University of Tennessee. The lawsuit comprised several occurrences of sexual assault perpetrated by (former) student-athletes. The victims accused the school of encouraging a negative campus culture that not only permitted the assault to take place but also failed to offer support to the victims.

Sexual harassment is widespread in the academic sector. An obvious reality is that sexual harassment and assault has long been a problem in higher education institutions, only that it has never been acknowledged.

In the past, there have been minor instances in the past in which a college or university has been caught up in a sexual misconduct scandal, but never to the extent of what's happening today.

The establishment of #metoo has compelled many industries, from hospitality to Hollywood to academia, to agree that sexual misconduct has been ignored severally for a long time.

The structure of academic institutions is partly to blame. Presently, most universities and colleges still use a very traditional and hierarchical structure. There departments of non-faculty members, junior professors, tenured professors, department chairs, deans and presidents in addition to differences in age, race, ethnicity, gender, and ability.

The structure of higher education is hierarchical and has very dependent relationships between faculty and trainees (e.g., students, postdoctoral fellows, residents). Finally, and especially in the fields of science, engineering, and medicine, academia often involves work or training in isolated environments.

Research has consistently proved that institutions that are male-dominated—with men in positions that can directly influence the career options of women who are subordinate to them have high rates of sexual harassment.

The manner in which roles are allocated and classified makes it tempting for those who have the power to take advantage of those in less powerful positions.

Some experts assert that harassment and secrecy may be even more prevalent in higher education institutions than other workplaces because of the "entrenched stratification and gendered hierarchies among faculty".

Additionally, the faculty structure also permits the existence of a "secret code" that works to keep cases of harassment from spreading and retains problematic people in power.

Because universities and colleges have mostly ignored sexual harassment and assault issues in the past, they've created the impression that this kind of misconduct is allowed. Through previous actions, most higher education institutions have indicated that victims who come forward may not be believed, they may not be supported and they may be retaliated against.

Colleges and universities have made it seem like perpetrators will face few or no consequences. Matter of fact, if the harasser is a professor, they may even be promoted instead of being confronted.

The United States has a strong, vibrant, and internationally recognized enterprise in science, engineering, and medicine. These fields provide rewarding and challenging careers that women are pursuing at higher rates than in previous years. But over the past few decades, new initiatives in colleges and universities have made a good impact by improving the recruitment, retention, and advancement of women in the fields of science, engineering, and medicine. These efforts are capable of improving gender diversity as students in the life sciences and in medical schools are reaching gender parity and engineering programs at some campuses are recording significant growth in women's enrollment.

Still, these accomplishments are at risk. As women increasingly venture into these fields, they face biases and barriers that slow down their participation and career advancement in science, engineering, and medicine. As in other historically male-dominated fields, whether in academia or not, sexual harassment is one of the most pervasive of these challenges.

Some of the most high-profile cases of sexual harassment in academia have occurred within the fields of science, engineering, and medicine. In 2017 alone, there were more than 97 allegations of sexual harassment at institutions of higher education covered in the media, and there are likely many more allegations that are being filed through confidential formal reporting processes.

Current research indicates that the academic environments in science, engineering, and medicine display characteristics that enable high levels of risk for sexual harassment to occur. Higher education, currently and historically, has been a male-dominated environment, with men occupying most powerful and authoritative positions.

The gender inequity and the resulting power differences between men and women in higher education institutions have been present for years, and while some fields and institutions have been making progress in closing this gap, it still exists. Not only are there fewer women than men in most science, engineering, and medical fields (at the undergraduate student, graduate study, postdoctoral trainee, and faculty levels), but men also hold more powerful positions in academia. That means most department chairs and deans are men. Most principal investigators are men. Most provosts and presidents are men. These facts are not meant to imply that all or even most men are perpetrators of sexual harassment, but that this situation of majority male leadership can, and has led to minimization, improper response, and failure to consider the issue of sexual harassment or specific incidents seriously. As a result, this underrepresentation of women in science, engineering, and medicine and in positions of leadership in these fields creates a high-risk environment for sexual harassment that can have a negative influence on women's education and careers.

The greatest factor that can predict the occurrence of sexual harassment is the organizational climate in a school, department, or program, or across an institution. Organizational climate for sexual harassment (also known as the perceptions of organizational tolerance) is evaluated based on three elements: (1) the perceived risk to those who report sexually harassing actions, (2) absence of sanctions against offenders, and (3) the assumption that one's report of sexually harassing behavior will not be taken seriously. In settings that are considered as more tolerant or permissive of sexual harassment, women are more likely to be directly harassed.

An environment that does not support harassing behaviors and/or has firm, clear, transparent consequences for these behaviors can greatly reduce the likelihood that sexual harassment will be perpetrated, even by people who are more likely to engage in sexually harassing behaviors.

Apart from these risk factors, there are also conditions in institutions that worsen the problem. They include:

• Insufficient attention to sexual harassment among campus leaders—including presidents, provosts, deans, and department chairs.

• Lack of clear policies and procedures in the institution, and within departments, that clearly state all forms of sexual harassment, including gender harassment, will not be tolerated; those investigations will be taken seriously; and that there are serious punishments for going against the policies.

• Minimal or merely symbolic compliance with the law without considering whether policies actually prevent harassment and retaliation.

• Lack of sufficient protection for targets of sexual harassment, who often face grave consequences when they report sexually harassing behavior.

• Lack of effective training on sexual harassment. Although nearly all institutions offer some form of "sexual harassment training," and often require all students, faculty, and staff to take the training, rarely is the training reviewed and revised to ensure that it has the expected effect of eliminating or preventing harassment.

• Measuring the problem of sexual harassment based on how many cases are formally reported to the institution, instead of conducting regular climate surveys.

• Insufficient attention to a climate that tolerates the gender harassment form of sexual harassment, which escalates the likelihood that other forms of sexual harassment will occur.

These conditions, which are present in most institutions can be addressed, and sexual harassment can be reduced, prevented and even permanently eliminated. More and more campuses are adopting policies and strategies that address the issue by focusing on altering the culture and climate in their departments, schools, and programs—and across the institution— resultantly creating environments where sexual harassment is less likely to occur.

Their objectives are to:

(1) Create learning environments that are inclusive, embrace diversity and are respectful as well.

(2) Diffuse the power structure and reduce isolation.

(3) Provide support to targets of sexual harassment and give them options for dealing with sexual harassment.

(4) Affirm that sexually harassing behavior is unacceptable.

(5) Confront and hold accountable those who engage in sexually harassing behavior.

As a way to deal with this issue, many institutions, schools, and departments are taking the following steps:

• Modifying hiring, promotion, and admission procedures to value and accept diversity, inclusion, and respectful behavior.

• Stabilizing and evaluating sexual harassment pieces of training, and integrating bystander intervention training.

• Altering funding and mentoring structures for trainees to reduce the power imbalance between them and faculty.

• Devising policies and procedures that give targets of harassment alternatives to speak with non-mandatory reporters and greater control over how and when they continue with their harassment case.

• Providing leadership development centered on equipping campus administrators with the tools they need to combat and handle sexual harassment.

• Publicizing anti-harassment policies and showing that people are being held accountable when they are proved to have violated the policies and thereby clearly affirming that sexual harassment is not tolerated.

If sexual harassment can be addressed using a systemic change to the culture and climate of institutions of higher education, there is the possibility to not only benefit women but also benefit men and another underrepresented groups. This move will later benefit the enterprise of science, engineering, and medicine. To accomplish such a systemic change requires identifying what does and does not work about the current education system and thinking creatively and unconventionally about ways to create new perspectives and evidence-based solutions to sexual harassment.

Higher education is also replete with incidents where offenders are an "open secret" but are not sanctioned. Interviews carried out by RTI International with female faculty in science, engineering, and medicine who experienced sexually harassing behavior, show some of the issues that describe this general climate of accepting sexual harassment. The interview responses reveal that the behavior of male colleagues, whom higher-ranking faculty or administrators considered as "superstars" in their particular substantive area, was mostly minimized or ignored. Even men who did not have the superstar label were often described as getting preferential treatment and excused for gender-biased and sexually harassing actions.

The normalization of sexual harassment and gender bias was also noted as encouraging this behavior in new cohorts of sciences, engineering, and medicine faculty. Respondents described the disheartening encounters of colleagues who entered training environments with nonbiased views and respectful behavior, but who concluded those experiences approving or ignoring sexually harassing and gender-biased behavior among themselves and others.

Expectations around behavior were often considered as an excuse for older generations of faculty, especially men, to engage in sexually harassing behavior. Many respondents stated that the "old guard," in perpetuating this type of behavior, was doing what they have always done and was not likely to change, due to a general acceptance within academic environments.

Sometimes it takes many reports across multiple organizations for a perpetrator's behavior to even be acknowledged. This reality, as well as the perspectives broadly held across higher education, means that few targets believe their allegations will be taken seriously.

Since many colleges and universities in America were established for the main purpose to educate men, higher education environments are also often historically male-dominated, and science, engineering, and medicine in higher education still remain numerically and culturally male-dominated. While women have earned more than half of all science and engineering bachelor's degrees since 2000, academic science and engineering as a whole have remained very male-dominated because of the high concentration of women in only a handful of specific scientific fields. As the National Science Foundation's 2016 Science and Engineering Indicators observes, men and women tend to enroll in different fields of study, and these tendencies are consistent at all levels of higher education degree attainment.

In 2013 alone, men earned 80.7 percent of bachelor's degrees awarded in engineering, 82 percent in computer sciences, and 80.9 percent in physics. On the other hand, women earned half or more of the bachelor's degrees in psychology, biological sciences, agricultural sciences, and all the broad fields within social sciences except for economics. Additionally, in biology-related fields where women make up more than one-half of all doctorate recipients, they are widely underrepresented at the faculty level. A 2014 study by Jason Sheltzer and Joan Smith published in the Proceedings of the National Academy of Sciences showed that of 2,062 life sciences faculty members at top-ranked programs in the United States, only 21 percent of full professors and 29 percent of assistant professors were women.

In medicine, although women have been earning medical degrees in numbers at least equal to men for several decades, female medical school faculty do not advance as fast and are not compensated as well as their male counterparts. A survey carried out by the Association of American Medical Colleges further indicates the disparities in career advancement between men and women: 1 in 6 department chairs or deans were women in 2013–2014, up from 1 in 10 in 2003–2004; 38 percent, only a little more than a third, of full-time academic medicine faculty, are women; and only 21 percent of full professors are women, as are 34 percent of full-time associate professors.

The culture of higher education workplaces, where boundaries between work and personal life are unclear and one is always working, is especially difficult on people with childcare or eldercare responsibilities, as well as for people who do not adhere to gendered expectations for behavior or appearance. These people are most often women and sexual- and gender minority people. Conventionally, the life of the mind was perceived to be men's work, and while our society may have more modern views today on the contributions of women to higher education generally and science specifically, the structure of the academic workplace is still one most appropriate for men who have a wife at home serving as domestic caretaker full time. That means the ideal worker norm is pervasive in academia.

In the medical sector, training specifically takes place in hospital settings, over 24-hour "call" periods. Interns and residents (even the nomenclature attest to the trainees having a special relationship to the hospital training space) offer most of the patient care under the direction of faculty attending physicians who may or may not be physically present in the hospital for the educational purposes. Taking care of sick patients, especially in the emergency room, the operating rooms and the intensive care units is often very intense, exhausting, and stressful, and because of the requirement for extended duty hours, call rooms with single or multiple beds are close by for the time when sleep is possible. The risk they pose for sexual harassment and sexual assault is great... Additional research on the medical environment indicates that overall "mistreatment" is commonplace in all levels of the medical hierarchy, especially among medical school students, interns, and residents in all specialties. When putting together, these environmental and mentoring factors mean that there are greater opportunities for sexual harassment perpetration, in environments with little structure or limited accountability for the faculty member, and a lower ability for students to leave without professional consequences.

In one of the most credible meta-analysis to date on sexual harassment prevalence, Ilies and colleagues (2003)

discovered that 58 percent of female academic faculty
and staff experienced sexual harassment. Apart from the
academic setting, the meta-analysis examines sexual
harassment in private-sector, government, and military
samples. When comparing the academic workplace with
the other workplaces, the survey revealed that the
academic workplace had the second-highest rate, behind
the military (69%). The government and private-sector
samples were very close to each other with 43 percent
and 46 percent, respectively. The top two workplaces
(the military and academia) are both more male-
dominated than the private sector and the government,
displaying the significance this has on rates of
harassment and also indicating that in areas of academia
that are more male-dominated (such as engineering and
specific science disciplines and specialties of medicine),
the rates of sexually harassing behavior are likely to be
higher.

In a more recent study of examining the experiences
of women and men working in academia, the court
system, and the military, the connection to male-
dominated workplaces was confirmed for academia. It

showed that even at a unit level when the underrepresentation of women increased one unit, the odds that women would face gender harassment increased 1.2 times. For female faculty and staff in academia, research has also confirmed the general finding from other workplaces that the majority of the sexual harassment experienced was gender harassment and that the other two types of sexual harassment were rarely experienced without gender harassment also occurring documented that this pattern—gender harassment being far more prevalent that other types of sexual harassment— still exists today. Their focus was on the experiences of graduate students, who in many ways can work as university employees. Their research found that "the majority of harassment experiences involved sexist or sexually offensive language, gestures, or photos (59.1%), with 6.4% involving unwanted sexual attention, 4.7% involving unwanted touching, and 3.5% involving subtle or explicit bribes or threats".

Sexual harassment can occur bottom-up, coming from those who have less formal power in the organization; researchers often define this as "contra power harassment." For instance, in 2000, O'Connell and Korabik reported that 42 percent of their sample of women working in academia (as faculty, staff, or administrators) had faced sexually harassing conduct from men at lower levels in the organizational hierarchy. Similar to many other studies, the majority of this subordinate-perpetrated harassment was gender harassment which involved insulting remarks about women, vulgar gestures, and lewd jokes.

Likewise, a 1989 report stated that 48 percent of women faculty at a large research university had experienced sexually harassing conduct from students; most commonly, this behavior involved sexist comments (defined as "jokes or remarks that are stereotypical or derogatory to members of your sex"). Virtually all instances (99 percent) involved men as perpetrators. In one case, the student-on-faculty sexual harassment advanced to rape. To describe the dynamics underlying contra power harassment, Grauerholz (1989) noted that "even in situations in which a woman has clearly defined authority, gender continues to be one of the most salient and powerful variables governing work relations." This is similar to Gutek and Morasch's (1982) concept of "sex-role spillover," which asserts that gender-based norms (i.e., woman as a maid, woman as nagging a mother) tend to extend into the workplace. In this way, contra power sexual harassment reflects the lower status of women (especially women of color) in society relative to men, and it replicates that hierarchy in organizations is highly significant.

Harassing behavior often includes sexual advances, lewd jokes or comments, disparaging or critical comments related to competency, unwanted sexual touching, stalking, and sexual assault by a colleague.

The prevalence of female undergraduates who experienced crude behavior and nonassault forms of unwanted sexual attention in the 2014–2015 academic year ranged from 14 percent to as high as 46 percent in some universities.

Sexual harassment can also be perpetrated by students on students. The Association of American University Women 2005 online survey, which used a Non-SEQ set of behavior-based questions that left out sexist comments and focused on sexual behavior, found that 62 percent of all undergraduates had encountered sexual harassment. The research includes questions about the perpetrator, and the results showed that at college-related events and activities, peer harassment was notably more common than harassment by faculty. 80 percent of students who were harassed reported it was from peers or former peers and only 18 percent reported it was perpetrated by faculty or staff.

A study conducted in 2015 by Clancy of 474 astronomers and planetary scientists observed that women who encountered sexist comments were more likely to be trainees (students) at the time and slightly more likely to experience it from peers or others at the same rank or level in the formal institutional hierarchy than from superiors. Similar to other findings, the women in this study were more likely than the men to report incidents of sexual harassment.

The study also questioned respondents about other forms of harassment including racial harassment and asked whether they felt insecure in their position because of either their gender or race. The study found that women were more likely than men to report feeling unsafe because of their gender (30 percent of women respondents versus 2 percent of men respondents) and that respondents of color were more likely to admit feeling unsafe because of their race (24 percent versus 1 percent of white respondents). Women of color were the most likely to experience verbal racial harassment (compared with men of color and white men and women), and that they were equally likely as white women to face verbal sexual harassment. In addition, women of color were most likely to report feeling unsafe compared with men of color, white women, or white men, and almost 1 in 2 women of color reported feeling unsafe because of their gender (40 percent based on gender and 28 percent based on race).

This study is similar to other research on women of color that indicates women of color experience more harassment (as a combination of sexual and racial harassment) and are therefore likely to be dealing with more negative experiences than other groups. Overall, this research complements the obvious evidence that white women and women of color in the astronomy and planetary science fields are facing sexual harassment at a level similar to other workplaces with similar environmental variables.

Field research is a significant part of scientific scholarship, but it is also an environment that can present higher risks for sexual harassment. A survey of academic field experiences (the SAFE study) pointed out systemic and problematic behaviors in scientific field sites that may lead to a hostile environment. The study listed multiple characteristics of field-site environments and the sexual harassment that occurs: (1) there was a lack of awareness concerning codes of conduct and sexual harassment policies, with few respondents being aware of available reporting mechanisms; (2) the victims of sexually harassing behavior in field sites were mostly women trainees, and (3) perpetrators varied between men and women—when women were harassed, perpetrators were primarily senior to the trainees; however, when men were harassed, it was often by a peer.

In 2014, Clancy and colleagues employed a snowball sampling technique to contact this diverse population of field scientists, and among those that responded, 64 percent (both men and women) had personally experienced sexual harassment in field sites in the form of offensive sexual remarks, comments about physical appearances or cognitive sex differences, or sexist or demeaning jokes, and more than 20 percent of respondents reported having personally experienced sexual assault. The research also observed that harassment and assault at field sites were primarily targeted at trainees (students and postdocs), and particularly, 90 percent of the women who were harassed were trainees or employees when they were targeted at the field site. Notably, the research found that in the field sites, women primarily experienced sexual harassment that was perpetrated by someone superior to them in the field-site hierarchy.

This higher likelihood of the harassment being perpetrated by superiors is clearly a unique characteristic that distinguishes research field sites from other workplace settings where it is more common for the harassment to be initiated by peers. This characteristic of field sites is significant in understanding the gravity of the sexual harassment experienced because the outcomes from sexual harassment can be worse if it comes from a superior who has authority or power over the target.

In a 2017 follow-up, the SAFE team conducted a thematic analysis of 26 interviews of women and men field scientists. The first observation of this paper was that respondents had very different experiences of field sites where rules were absent, where they were present, and where they were present and implemented. That is, those field sites with high organizational tolerance for sexual harassment—field sites without rules, or those with rules but the rules were not enforced—were ones where respondents narrated sexual harassment and assault experiences. The second observation was that the scientists who were sexually harassed or experienced other incivilities had worse career experiences, which is also similar to the broader workplace aggression literature. Finally, the authors found that egalitarian field sites were ones that set a good example for scientists, had fewer incivilities, sexual harassment experiences, and sexual assault, and created positive experiences for respondents that reaffirmed their commitment to science. These data exhibit a way forward, in the sense that organizational antecedents for sexual harassment in science work and education settings match with those of other workplaces, and that therefore the literature provides strong, evidence-based recommendations for eliminating sexual harassment in science.

In research that has reviewed different specialties in medicine, female surgeons and physicians in specialties that are historically male-dominated are more likely to be harassed than those in other specialties, but only when they are in training. Once they finish their residency and enter in practice they experience harassment at the same rates as other specialties. This review suggested that for women in surgery and emergency medicine the higher rates of sexual harassment might be so due to those fields having and valuing a hierarchical and authoritative workplace. The preponderance of men in surgery and emergency medicine, and especially among leaders, is also likely a major factor in explaining the high harassment in these fields.

In two other studies, students perceived the experiences to be more common in the general surgery specialty than in others; and the other research shows that respondents reported their perceptions of these harassing settings influenced their choice in a specialty. Other studies suggest that sexual harassment may be worse depending on the medical setting; for example, women perceived sexual harassment and gender discrimination to be more prevalent in academic medical centers than in community hospitals and outpatient office settings.

One important observation from the research on the environment of academic medical centers is that in addition to students, trainees, and faculty being harassed by colleagues and those in leadership, they are also reporting harassment initiated by patients and patients' families. The studies showing this also suggest that harassment from patients and patients' families is very common and one of the top sources of the harassment they experience. This inappropriate behavior by patients and patients' families should be recognized by leaders in academic medical centers, and specific statements and punishments regarding sexual harassment should be included in the "Rights and Responsibilities" that are frequently presented to patients and families as they enter into both hospital and outpatient care in academic medical centers.

Research on students in high school who have experienced harassment shows that they report lowered motivation to attend classes, display greater truancy, pay less attention in class, attain lower grades on assignments and in their overall grade point average, and seriously contemplate changing schools. Even young women who have not been harassed avoid taking classes from teachers with reputations for being linked to harassing behavior.

At the undergraduate level, sexual harassment (of which the most common type is gender harassment), has adverse consequences on the educational path of students. For instance, the more often women students are harassed, the lower their assessments of the campus environment and the likelihood of returning to the college or university if they had to make the decision again. Furthermore, sexually harassed students have reported dropping classes, changing advisors, changing majors, and even dropping out of school altogether just to be away from hostile environments.

If women feel that the academic environment is hostile toward them, they may not take part in informal activities that could better their experiences and aid academic advancement. Sexual harassment can also have an impact on a student's self-esteem. This shows that low levels of academic involvement, performance, and motivation offer explanations as to why sexual harassment is associated with poor academic performance among female college students.

The more often women go through sexual harassment, the more they report symptoms of depression, stress and anxiety, and generally impaired psychological well-being.

Sexual harassment experiences by graduate students were associated with posttraumatic symptoms for both men and women. Female graduate students who conceded that they had experienced sexual harassment also reported a minimal sense of safety on campus. The University of Texas analysis of the ARC3 data suggests that across academic disciplines women who faced sexual harassment perpetrated by faculty/staff reported noticeably worse physical and mental health outcomes than those who had not experienced sexual harassment.

Other psychological outcomes of sexual harassment include:

- Negative moods
- Fear
- Eating disorders
- Self-blame, low self-esteem
- Increased use of prescription drugs
- Anger, disgust
- Lower satisfaction with life in general

The tangible losses women deal with as a result of harassment can include the loss of a job and its associated economic, personal, and social benefits. Among these, loss of income and economic security is often the most adverse. Women experiencing sexual harassment also incur intangible but significantly great losses. They often lose self-esteem and confidence in themselves and their competency, and they often report loss of motivation or passion for their work. Additionally, distractions and loss of significant relationships, inside and outside the workplace or academic community, are common. These can comprise loss of important mentoring or coworker relationships and tension on family and social relationships, including relationships with intimate partners and social networks.

The disruption and loss of these relationships can deprive women of this support and can exacerbate the psychological and physical outcomes.

If harassment leads to stigmatization and the loss of a greatly valued training opportunity or career, the impact on the target can be devastating, beyond the financial stresses associated with the loss of a job. When a woman has made a personal, professional, and financial commitment to and investment in highly specialized science, engineering, and medical training, such as deciding to forego having children or investing years in "paying dues" to advance in her profession, the loss of a training or employment position results in profound grief.

Even if she is able to leave the environment in which the harassment has taken place, a "reputation" may prevent the woman from being enrolled in the limited similar training programs or obtaining the few available positions in science, engineering, and medicine.

When compared with the research on psychological health outcomes, the literature on physical health outcomes is less extensive and seems to be indirect, which means emerging as a result of its connection to psychological health. In other words, women who are going through psychological distress may report stress-related physical complaints as well. Some studies have documented links to overall health perceptions or satisfaction.

Others have pointed out specific somatic complaints resulting from harassing experiences; which include headaches, exhaustion, sleep problems, gastric problems, nausea, respiratory complaints, musculoskeletal pain, and weight loss/gain.

Specifically, one experiment has shown a causal connection between gender harassment, the most common form of sexual harassment, and physiological measures of stress. When women were subjected to sexist comments from a male coworker, they experienced cardiac and vascular activity similar to that exhibited in threat situations. This kind of cardiovascular reactivity has been linked to coronary heart disease and depressed immune functioning. The researchers conclude that if women are exposed to persistent, long-term gender harassment and the resulting physical stress, they could be at risk for serious long-term health problems.

Although all types of sexual harassment will have negative effects, top-down sexual harassment (i.e., carried out by a superior) is sometimes more devastating than peer harassment. For instance, studies have shown that working women who experience sexual harassment from higher-level men, rather than equal or lower-level men, face greater impacts and negative outcomes for targets' job satisfaction, intent to leave one's job, and organizational commitment, as well as health-related variables such as depression, emotional exhaustion, and physical well-being.

Furthermore, research has observed that the more powerful the perpetrator, the more that women find his harassing conduct distressing. Huerta and colleagues' (2006) study of college students reported that academic satisfaction was lower when the harassment came from higher-status individuals (i.e., faculty, staff, or administrators).

Ambient sexual harassment is described as the indirect exposure to sexual harassment or "the general or ambient level of sexual harassment in a workgroup as measured by the frequency of sexually harassing behaviors faced by others in a woman's workgroup". It will lead to similar negative outcomes as direct exposure. Organizational stressors such as racial harassment and organizational politics are proved to cause heightened stress to employees who are not themselves targets. In this study, experts propose that such research suggests that "effects of job stressors are quite diffuse and extend beyond the focal target". Ambient sexual harassment in the workplace has a detrimental effect on an employee's job satisfaction and psychological conditions. According to authentic findings, women who experience sexual harassment, directly and indirectly, report higher levels of absenteeism and intentions to quit, and are more likely to leave work early, go on long breaks, and skip meetings (job withdrawal).

Sexual and gender minority individuals, an often overlooked group, can also be affected by the impact of sexual harassment differently. A study by Irwin (2002) reports that the impact on health and well-being to gender minorities is shocking, with 90 percent of those in the sample stating that they experienced heightened anxiety and stress levels while at work.

Sexual harassment does not only impact the target but may also affect employees and coworkers who witness or hear about the experience. Several studies have endeavored to document these effects to show that negative impacts associated with indirect experiences of sexual harassment will also affect other women (and men) in the victim's workgroup or team.

All employees in an institution—whether female and male—can suffer from working in a setting perceived to be hostile toward women. As a result, the concept of ambient sexual harassment has far-reaching implications for organizations. The studies above confirm that sexual harassment is not only a personal problem but also an organizational problem.

The varying layers of an individual's identity may affect the way one perceives and deals with sexual harassment in the workplace or academia.

Some women are forced to make major transitions in their careers as a result of these experiences. Three themes emerged from this observation regarding the impacts on their job opportunities, advancement, and tenure: stepping down from leadership opportunities to avoid the perpetrator, leaving their institution, and leaving their field altogether.

These responses to sexual harassment deprive an institution of many talented women and limit their ability to advance and contribute to the work in particular fields.

Certain analyses of the ARC3 data from the University of Texas System indicate that there are some differences between academic disciplines in the outcomes from going through sexually harassing behavior. Female students in medical school, in the sciences, and in non-SEM fields who were harassed by faculty/staff reported feeling less safe on campus than those who had not been targets of sexual harassment.

Female engineering students were the only exception and did not report feeling less safe than those who had not been sexually harassed. Female science majors and non-SEM majors who experienced any sexual harassment by faculty or staff reported similar academic disengagement results —reporting missing class, being late for class, making excuses to leave class, and submitting poor work—significantly more often than those who did not experience sexual harassment, while female engineering majors who experienced any sexual harassment by faculty or staff were only significantly more likely to report missing more classes and making more excuses to leave classes than their peers who had not experienced harassment.

Across the fields in academic science, engineering, and medicine, there is high value attached to not only on your Ph.D. or M.D. institution but also on the lab, program, or hospital you are from. The status of your institutional affiliation and advisor greatly influences your chances of obtaining a tenure-track faculty position, specifically at an R1 institution. In this setting, specific aspects of the science, engineering, and medicine academic workplace tend to silence targets as well as limit career opportunities for both victims and bystanders.

Informal communication networks known as "whisper networks,"14 in which rumors and accusations are circulated within and across specialized programs and fields, are common across many male-dominated work and education environments, including science, engineering, and medicine. Informal communication networks designed by and for women are used to warn women away from particular programs, labs, or advisors. This has the effect of automatically limiting their options and chances for career success. Still, this protective type of networking is common and referenced by many women who experience sexually harassing behaviors and settings.

These informal communication networks may have the purpose of protecting women from harassment, but they also limit opportunities. When a female graduate student or postdoc finds herself going through sexual harassment, she has few choices to separate herself from the perpetrator or perpetrators aside from leaving that program or lab. This puts her at a detrimental disadvantage: if she leaves that program or lab, she may have no other options at that institution to do similar work. Eventually, her options are to start a whole new line of research or apply to a new Ph.D. program. This shows why women who experience sexual harassment in the sciences often report lateral career moves, taking lesser jobs, continuing a working relationship with their perpetrator, or quitting science altogether. Female medical students who encountered any sexual harassment perpetrated by faculty or staff were only significantly more likely to report submitting poor work than their peers who had not experienced sexual harassment.

Laws and Policies Against Harassment

The development of law and policies about sexual harassment in academic settings started in the 1970s, first with the passage of Title IX in 1972 (part of the Education Amendments of 1972), banning discrimination on the basis of sex under any education program or activity receiving federal funds, and later with judicial interpretations of Title VII of the Civil Rights

Act of 1964, prohibiting sex discrimination and including harassment as part of discrimination. Title IX applies to academic institutions receiving federal assistance, including financial aid for students (such as student loans), and bars the discrimination (which includes harassment) of those seeking education. Title VII discrimination protections are based on employment status. Women in academic science, engineering, and medicine fields may be students, employees, or in both categories at the same time.

Title IX protections in education developed before the term "sexual harassment" had been invented, but it proceeded out of activist mobilization from groups such as the National Organization for Women and congressional energy around the Equal Rights Amendment. The first legislative movement came under the instructions of Representative Edith Green from Oregon, whose work on the Subcommittee on Higher Education came up with evidence documenting widespread discrimination on the basis of sex in education. During that period, for example, women were not admitted as students to many colleges and universities (even public universities) or were denied readmission after marriage. In an effort for change, Senator Birch Bayh of Indiana took a provision of the delayed Equal Rights Amendment and introduced it as an amendment to the Higher Education Act of 1965, later renamed the Patsy T. Mink Equal Opportunity in Education Act in honor of House coauthor Representative Patsy Mink of Hawai'i.

Title IX has become well known for its transformations of athletic opportunities for women and girls in the field of education, but its main principle is equal opportunity for men and women to seek and to complete their education. Courts use interpretations of sex discrimination established under Title VII (the employment law) for Title IX, and so as sexual harassment law developed under Title VII, it also applied under Title IX. Though the details of institutional obligations have been controversial and may change under different presidential administrations, it has been a legal principle for decades that allowing harassment on the basis of sex to close off access to educational opportunities for youth or adults violates Title IX.

Feminist scholars shifted both the legal doctrine of sexual harassment as well as administrative plans for changing organizational climates to combat it. Most significantly, they stated that sexual harassment amounted to illegal sex discrimination under Title VII of the 1964 Civil Rights Act. Feminist scholars also drew up detailed organizational policy recommendations. Backhouse and Cohen (1978), Canadian feminists with careers in government and in business, published a management action plan in 1978 that recommended the core elements of organizational response commonly used today, such as a strong policy statement from top leaders against sexual harassment; clear policy defining it and stating that it is unacceptable in the workplace; posting and publication throughout company manuals and publications; trainings; oversight procedures, including surveying employees; protecting targets from retaliation; and a complaint and disciplinary procedure for addressing complaints. By 1980 the Equal Employment Opportunity Commission (EEOC) issued guidelines supporting both MacKinnon's legal remedy and Backhouse and Cohen's recommended organizational responses, and courts and other federal agencies approved the guidelines.

Title VII of the 1964 Civil Rights Act and Title IX of the Education Amendments in effect work collectively to protect employees and students, respectively, from discrimination. Title VII majors on the protection of employees from discrimination based on an individual's race, color, religion, sex (including sexual harassment by judicial interpretation and pregnancy by amendment), or national origin. Sexual harassment under Title VII is classified into two varieties: quid pro quo harassment (conditioning some feature of a target's job on sexual performance or submission) and hostile environment harassment.

Both Title VII and Title IX are relevant in academic settings, sites of both employment and education. Institutional compliance with both laws has taken the form of widespread adoption of policies and procedures to address sexual harassment complaints (as a form of sex discrimination) and to inform employees and students of these policies and procedures. In contrast, with Title VII (under which these policies are recommended and widely adopted but not required under the statute), Title IX specifically requires the designation of an employee to organize compliance, adoption, and publication of a grievance procedure, and widespread notification that it does not discriminate. The legal regime of sexual harassment, therefore, incorporates the major pieces of federal legislation (Title VII and Title IX), but also their judicial interpretations as developed through case law; regulations, guidelines, and letters from each administrative agency in charge of implementing the statutes; and the internal claims filing and resolution processes in place across organizations.

All forms of sexually harassing behavior, whether or not the conduct is sexual in nature (for example, sexist hostility that is not sexual), can be classified as illegal forms of harassment if they occur "because of sex" and meet the bar for severity or pervasiveness. Title IX addresses sex discrimination in educational programs or activities at institutions receiving federal assistance (including financial aid, meaning that it is relevant in nearly all colleges and universities). The Department of Education materials from 2008 define sexual harassment

under Title IX as "conduct that is sexual in nature; is
unwelcome, and denies or limits a student's ability to
participate in or benefit from a school's education
program".

Even if the descriptions of sexual harassment are
similar under the two laws, Title IX and Title VII have
different approaches to institutional liability for sexual
harassment. According to Title IX, an educational
institution must have been "deliberately indifferent" in
the face of actual knowledge of the harassment. On the
other hand, Title VII's initial standard of liability for
employers is much stronger but is tempered by a
generous affirmative defense against hostile environment
complaints. In 1998, two Supreme Court cases,
Burlington Industries, Inc. v. Ellerth2 and Faragher v.
City of Boca Raton,3 clarified the nature of legal liability
in Title VII sexual harassment cases. An employer is
vicariously (or automatically) liable for a supervisor's
sexual harassment if the harassed employee experienced
a visible harm such as a demotion, firing, failure to get
promotion or, in the academic context, such harms as
exclusion from a research site or lab; restrictions from

using data; or withdrawal of promised fellowship support (these are examples of outcomes of quid pro quo harassment).

The Department of Education's Office for Civil Rights (OCR) is the federal office responsible for upholding Title IX. According to OCR, an institution's sexual harassment grievance procedures must be "prompt and equitable." A proper policy must integrate the following:

• Give notice to students, faculty, and staff of the procedure and where complaints may be filed;

• Provide information about how procedures will be carried out when the sexual harassment involves employees, other students, or third parties;

• Provide an adequate, reliable, and impartial investigation of the complaint, with the opportunity to present witnesses and other evidence;

• Devise a response within a reasonable amount of time, give notice to all parties about the outcome of the complaint; and

- Take action to prevent recurrence of any harassment and to correct its discriminatory effects on the complainant and others, if necessary.

This 2001 Revised Sexual Harassment Guidance document still remains in place.

Legal scholars and scholars of organizations have been very critical of the incentives and assumptions approved under the legal response to sexual harassment. The incentive is to avoid liability by drawing up policies and procedures, and the assumption is that targets will quickly and vigorously utilize them. Strict liability means that a court only needs to confirm that the harassment occurred with tangible harm to the harassed person's working conditions (i.e., there is no separate investigation into whether the employing college or university was negligent). Employers are accountable for a hostile work environment resulting from sexual harassment only if they were negligent, however—that is, if they knew or should have known about the harassment and took no action to stop it. In other instances, employers could conceivably distance themselves from liability completely without provoking a change in the underlying problem. These liability standards in both the Title IX and Title VII context together with the organizational response can help explain the empirical trends observed in many studies - policies against sexual harassment are widely recognized and have been in place for many years, but nonetheless, sexual harassment in academic institutions continues to persist and has not been eliminated.

Scholars of law and organizations have discovered that in recent decades, large bureaucratic organizations such as colleges and universities are quasi governments for themselves; that is, a college or university typically coordinates its own police or security forces; conducts internal grievance and dispute resolution procedures; dispenses punishments and sanctions; manages public relations and information services; and appoints in-house counsel staffs as well as administrators to oversee this legal order. The college or university is likely also the health care and psychological support services provider for students and perhaps even employees. Since very few disputes end up in the courts, these academic legal orders will deal with the majority of problems internally.

Therefore, there are several legally significant features of these academic environments that extend far beyond sexual harassment law but which have major implications for addressing harassment, particularly for promoting transparency about how harassment claims are handled. Transparency about outcomes may be legally required, permitted, or prohibited depending on the type of conduct (harassment that is also criminal versus noncriminal harassment), the status of the parties (students or employees), and the type of information (an outcome of an adjudication, a complaint, a personnel document, or a police report.

For example, private academic institutions are able to protect their personnel decisions, adjudication outcomes, and financial matters from the public eye, but state public records laws (variable, but modeled after the federal Freedom of Information Act) apply to public state colleges and universities. Additionally, the Higher Education Act of 1965 compels consumer-based disclosures by institutions that benefit from federal funds (information about admissions, graduation rates, costs, financial aid, student services, among others).

Academic employers may also be sued for invasion of privacy tort claims if they disclose embarrassing information about someone, and colleagues may hesitate to warn about sexual harassment concerns in the hiring or promotion context out of fear of being sued for defamation. Confidentiality agreements in settlements will also hide harassment cases from scrutiny and make it possible for perpetrators to apply for new jobs and keep problems secret.

The Clery Act) also applies to all institutions receiving federal funds and requires them to report crimes near or on campus, including sexual assaults. While the Clery Act instructs all institutions to report a crime, state open records laws may require only public institutions to disclose full campus police incident reports, for example. The Family Educational Rights and Privacy Act of 1974 protect the privacy of student records, including disciplinary actions, though after a finding against a perpetrator of a sex offense, the results of that proceeding may be revealed. In accordance with the Health Insurance Portability and Accountability Act, the Family and Medical Leave Act, and the Americans with Disabilities Act, academic employers are subject to privacy laws governing medical information and information on employees' disabilities and accommodations, and may also be subject to state law prohibitions on revealing information from a personnel file (such as past sexual harassment accusations).

The legal mechanisms in place to protect women from sexual harassment, and to respond to sexual harassment once it has taken place, have major limitations. Any serious attempt to address sexual harassment through the law, through institutional policies or procedures, or through cultural change should at a minimum take into account the social science research showing that targets of sexual harassment are not likely to report and that there are more effective practices to enforce policies on sexual harassment. The mandatory arbitration clauses that are standard in many employment contracts also prevent women from reporting sexual harassment claims in federal courts, handing them over to a faster and less costly arbitration system that hides the case from scrutiny and results in smaller awards.

Title IX is best known for its significant social impacts in expanding women's opportunities in sport, including in academia. Any academic institution that receives federal support must follow the requirements of Title IX. In practice, this means that almost all academic institutions must implement the requirements of this law, which has only relatively recently been visible as the main way to respond to sexual assaults and sexual harassment on campus. Colleges and universities have been under pressure to put up policies and procedures governing the prevention of and response to sexual harassment, but just as under Title VII, it is much more difficult to ensure that such policies and procedures are impactful or user-friendly. Additionally, research has indicated that compliance with Title IX requirements is inconsistent, with several institutions failing to meet even the low bar set by the legal requirements.

Many institutions have closely reviewed their policies and revised them with the aim of improving responsiveness and providing more options for recourse. For instance, in the wake of a series of high-profile sexual harassment incidents where those in leadership positions did not follow up on reports of sexual harassment, the University of California system has now specified that all members of the Title IX team have clearly identified roles and responsibilities in managing all processes related to occurrences of sexual harassment. In addition, a timeline that makes sure that all investigations are completed within 60 business days must be in place, and a decision or disciplinary action must be defined within 40 days after the end of the investigation. Any recommended disciplinary action must be revised and approved by a chancellor or chancellor-designee. Once decisions have been made, all complainants and respondents will be informed of any results or outcomes.

For every victim of sexual harassment, social support inside and/or outside the institution is one of the most elemental factors that can alleviate the stress and trauma sexual harassment causes.

CHAPTER SEVEN: SEXUAL HARASSMENT IN THE MILITARY

Men and women are both targets of sexual assault perpetrated by members of the military service. About 25 percent of female veterans who seek health care services from the Department of Veteran's Affairs report experiencing at least one incidence of sexual assault while in the military in comparison to more than 1 percent of male veterans. Women who enroll early in the military, at a young age, those of enlisted rank, and those who went through assault before enrolling in the military are often at a higher risk of facing assault during their time in the military.

Sexual assault in the American military increased in the last two years, characterized almost entirely by a 50 percent rise in assaults on women in uniform, according to a recent survey released by the Defense Department. The department's annual Report on Sexual Assault in the

Military indicated that there were 20,500 instances of "unwanted sexual contact" in the 2018 fiscal year, according to a survey of men and women across the Army, Navy, Air Force and Marines. That report showed an increase of 38 percent from the earlier survey in 2016.

Women now make up only about 20 percent of the military, but surprisingly, they are the targets of 63 percent of assaults, the survey found, with the youngest and lowest-ranking women at the greatest risk.

Overall, one out of every 16 military women reported being groped, raped or in another way sexually assaulted within the previous year. The survey found that while assaults on men in the military remained at the same rates, assaults on women recorded the highest increase in years.

A separate report in January observed that the number of sexual assaults at the nation's service academies had gone up by 50 percent since 2016, demonstrating that the problem is just as widespread among the military's future leaders as it is in the current ranks. Furthermore, it was closely similar to high rates reported at civilian colleges and universities.

The military-wide survey data released months ago shows that alcohol use has been a persistent contributing factor, and was to blame for 62 percent of assaults on women.

Incidents of assaults became higher across all branches, but the Marine Corps, which has proportionally more young, low-ranking troops and far fewer women than the other services, reported the highest rates. One in 10 surveyed women in the Marines claimed to be assaulted, twice the rate of either the Army or the Air Force.

Although the Pentagon has allocated hundreds of millions of dollars into prevention efforts, education programs and resources for victims in recent years, the issue still exists. There are many sexual assault specialists and victims' advocates, and the Army has even developed a hologram of an assault victim to assist with training.

Targets of sexual assault in the military rarely report their unpleasant experiences due to shame, fear, embarrassment and many other reasons, similar to those perceived by targets outside of the military. Additionally, there is less separation between a person's private and professional lives in the military. This builds up fear that other people will find out and the victims would be considered weak and lacking the capacity to achieve their mission. Some victims fear speaking out may affect assignments to better jobs, hinder promotion or even result in separation from the military.

A victim of sexual assault in the military may make a "restricted report" that permits disclosure to specified individuals (i.e., sexual assault response coordinator (SARC), sexual assault prevention and response victim advocate (SAPR VA), or healthcare personnel). The victim can access medical treatment, including emergency care, counseling, and assignment of a SARC and SAPR VA, without initiating an official investigation. Nevertheless, exceptions limit the ability to make a restricted report.

A victim may also make an "unrestricted report" without asking for confidentiality or restricted reporting. In this situation, the victim's report provided to healthcare personnel, the SARC, a SAPR VA, command authorities, or other persons is reported to law enforcement and may be used to start the official investigative process.

When an unrestricted report is filed, the alleged offender's commanding officer has a very high discretion about what action to take. He/she may take disciplinary, administrative, or legal action against the offender. He/she may also opt to administratively separate the service member from the military. Similar to the civilian system, many people feel that sexual assault offenders in the military are mostly not held accountable, which has the negative outcomes of minimizing, excusing, and condoning sexual assault and reinforcing sexist attitudes and behavior toward women.

The military has the capacity to and sometimes does take disciplinary or legal action against sexual assault survivors for infractions committed linked to the sexual assault (underage drinking, fraternization, adultery). Additionally, survivors have been separated from the military for mental health or disciplinary reasons, and they have limited recourse when this happens. This and other negative actions aimed at survivors are often considered as retaliation for reporting and can have adverse effects on the survivor's sense of safety, trust, and well-being and contribute to a complex string of problems that affect the survivor's future significantly even after leaving the military.

Congress has taken many legislative actions through the National Defense Authorization Act over the past several years to stabilize and improve the response to sexual assault in the military. The Department of Defense has also made many policy-related changes. Still, some have argued that unless the prosecution decision-making power is taken out of the hands of commanding officers, other changes will not influence the type of systemic and cultural changes that are necessary to end sexual assault in the military.

Sexual assault survivors who are in active duty have access to health and mental health care within the military system. There is a Sexual Assault Prevention and Response Program guided by Department of Defense regulations on each installation. Every command has a SARC and SAPR Vas available to offer advocacy and support for survivors. When a person leaves the military, services for sexual assault survivors are provided within the Department of Veterans Affairs and in community-based programs.

Sexual assault survivors often face myriad long-term health and mental health consequences from that trauma. They are likely to struggle with anger, guilt, shame, inability to trust, self-blame, etc. They often experience mental health issues such as post-traumatic stress disorder (PTSD), other anxiety disorders, depression, and substance abuse. This can result in unemployment, homelessness, disruption of interpersonal relationships, further victimization, physical problems, and suicide.

Military sexual trauma (MST) is psychological trauma, which in the judgment of a VA mental health professional, resulted from a physical assault of a sexual nature, battery of a sexual nature, or sexual harassment which occurred while the veteran was serving on active duty or active duty for training.

The Department of Veterans Affairs is the largest health care system in the country. Not all veterans are eligible for VA benefits and health and mental health care from the VA. They are expected to meet the VA eligibility requirements. Survivors of military sexual assault include both male and female veterans, but nearly a quarter of women veterans who seek health care from the VA report encountering at least one sexual assault while in the military.

The VA has appointed MST Coordinators at all VA medical centers throughout the country. Presently, the VA provides full health care for mental and physical health conditions connected to MST without any charges. Veterans do not need to have a service-connected disability or be seeking disability compensation to be eligible for MST-related counseling and care. Veterans are also not required to have reported such incidents to the Department of Defense or possess documentation or records to support their claim of having experienced such trauma.

The determination of whether a veteran's condition is MST-related is strictly a clinical determination made by the responsible VA mental health provider. And lastly, veterans don't need to enroll in VA's health care system to access MST-related treatment, since it is independent of VA's general treatment authority.

Through the VA, survivors can receive a variety of services to address needs related to their experiences of violence, including medical and mental health care, trauma-informed therapies, and links to supportive social work services for housing and employment counseling. Women veterans have the benefit of access to both community-based civilian services and VA-based services. Community-based civilian services may offer more specialized trauma-informed care. VA-based services may be more sensitive to the specific needs of women veterans and may be able to connect patients to care both within and outside the VA. Still, women veterans are not always comfortable requesting services from the VA and do not always consider the VA as being favorable to women veterans.

The threshold for documentation needed to ascertain eligibility for VA disability compensation for PTSD related to MST is presently higher than what is required for combat-related PTSD. This leads to many MST survivors being denied VA disability compensation for the sexual trauma and co-related health and mental health conditions that are mostly part of what follows after sexual assault.

CHAPTER EIGHT: EFFECTIVE SEXUAL HARASSMENT TRAINING

Although sexual harassment training is the most traditional measure employed to prevent sexual harassment, it has not been shown to completely combat the problem. The scholarship on effective sexual harassment training is sparse, but it clearly observes that, as indicated in the 2016 EEOC report, most of the training done over the last 30 years has not worked as a prevention tool—it's been too focused on simply evading legal liability.

When institutional sexual harassment pieces of training are rarely evaluated for their effectiveness, they have displayed mixed outcomes depending on what purpose they are being evaluated for. For example, several reports in the public domain, including the 2016 EEOC Task Force report, have shown that there is no evidence that training helps prevent harassment.

However, another goal of most sexual harassment training programs is to change employees' knowledge about the nature of, and organizations' policies about, sexual harassment.

In a sample of managers, sexual harassment training was closely associated with over-sensitization of identifying scenarios as sexual harassment, although there was no effect on precise identification of how to respond to the scenarios. A critical review of published studies on sexual harassment training effectiveness by Roehling and Huang (2018) revealed that sexual harassment training is relatively consistent in dispensing the knowledge of sexual harassment and internal reporting of perceived sexual harassment. Nevertheless, it observes that it is not clear to what extent knowledge attained during training is retained and applied in real-life scenarios.

While improving knowledge about sexual harassment and policies and procedures for reporting it are essential for assisting people to use those systems, the research does not prove that this kind of training is reducing or preventing sexual harassment. This is in part because knowledge and a change of attitude do not predict behavior change accurately, and reducing sexual harassment requires changes in behaviors.

A bigger challenge is that very few training programs are even evaluated for their impact on behavior change. A 2013 meta-analysis discovered how uncommon it is to evaluate pieces of training for their capacity to alter behaviors—only six of the studies in the meta-analysis of diversity and sexual harassment pieces of training examined actual behavioral change. And in what could be termed as the most important outcome for training— reduction in sexual harassment—one study revealed that training did not reduce sexual harassment.

Attitudes are highly resistant to change. Even worse, there was a backlash effect of a brief training intervention for one sample of men such that, after the training, they were more likely to blame a target of sexual harassment than those who did not receive the training. Another finding also suggests that policy training on harassment has the capacity to trigger gender stereotypes and backlash against women, especially in the administration of mandatory non-customized training.

Taken together, the set of studies on sexual harassment pieces of training shows that training can improve knowledge of policies and awareness of what is sexual harassment; nevertheless, pieces of training have either no effect or a negative effect on preventing sexual harassment.

Because changing behavior has more of a direct connection to reducing sexual harassment, that actions can be taken to prevent sexually harassing behavior even among those that hold sexist attitudes or beliefs that rationalize or justify harassment, and that changing attitudes is hard, effort seems better spent on developing and using sexual harassment trainings designed to change people's behaviors instead of their attitudes and beliefs. In the end, it is an individual's actions and behaviors that harm targets and are illegal, not their perceptions.

To determine how to conduct training so that it increases the likelihood that it will provide knowledge and change behavior, the research on diversity pieces of training can provide some insights. A meta-analysis of diversity and sexual harassment trainings concluded that whether such training improves knowledge, beliefs, or behaviors depends on several factors, including how the training was delivered, who conducted the training, where it was delivered, for whom it was delivered, why it was delivered, and the expected outcome of the training. This simply means that the context of the training is very important. This research concludes that positive effects are most likely to be witnessed when training:

- Was carried out for more than 4 hours,
- Was conducted face to face,
- Included active participation with other trainees on interdependent tasks,
- Was specifically customized for the audience, and
- Was conducted by a supervisor or an external expert.

The organizational context around the training can also have an impact on effectiveness. Three recent studies on sexual harassment pieces of training have suggested that the organizational context affects the efficacy of the training. First, knowledge and personal attitudes were changed for employees who believed that their work unit was ethical, regardless of their personal sense of cynicism about whether the training might be effective. Second, in a sample of untrained employees, perceptions that their organization tolerated sexual harassment affected employees' cynicism about the success of possible training, even more so than their own personal opinions about sexual harassment, which in turn influenced their motivation to learn from the possible training.

Third, in a meta-analysis of sexual harassment pieces of training, it's been established that training can contribute to the prevention or reduction of sexual harassment if "(a) it is carried out in accordance with science-based training principles and (b) the organizational context supports the sexual harassment training efforts." Based on their examination of the theory and empirical findings of sexual harassment literature, analysts Roehling and Huang have devised a conceptual framework for organizing and understanding the impact of sexual harassment training and the primary factors that interact to influence it. The major factors include:

- Training objectives
- Training design and delivery

- Trainee characteristics
- Organizational context (aligned policies and practices, leadership support, climate, and culture)
- Proximal outcomes (reactions, knowledge, skills, attitudes, perceived organizational tolerance of sexual harassment)
- Intermediate outcomes (incidence of sexual harassment, responses to sexual harassment)
- Distal outcomes (litigation, productivity, turnover)

Furthermore, in order to ensure the success of training in general, it is essential that it be based on the organization's identified needs—that is, aligned with the goals and objectives of the organization and the degree to which the elimination of harassment advances those goals and objectives—and, is itself one of those goals. This should be discussed together with sexual harassment training. Conducting a needs assessment, designing training centered on those needs, and then carefully evaluating its success have long been perceived to be the three fundamental elements of successful training.

The needs analysis should be based on gathering data from all employees and include, minimally, an estimate of the prevalence of sexual harassment within the organization, the extent to which supervisors are believed to tolerate sexual harassment, and existing knowledge about reporting procedures.

Another minimal pre-training criterion to include in the assessment of specific needs is employees' motivation to learn, considering that the general training literature shows its importance as influencing the success of intervention efforts.

Numerous studies have proved that motivation to learn is a key factor that influences short-term outcomes, which include reactions, knowledge and skill acquisition, and transfer. When trainees are more motivated to learn, better training outcomes are generally evident. When the goals of the training are considered, it could also include employees' general attitudes about sexual harassment and indicators of employees' professional and emotional well-being, to connect with their experiences of harassment. It's important for a needs analysis to consider data from employees, not on presumptions from human resource personnel or senior management.

Finally, the needs analysis should directly link to the evaluation plan associated with the training. Evaluation should be frequently expected as one of the components of the intervention, not as an additional burden; such evaluation would replicate the earlier needs assessment to show the change in sexual harassment, climate perceptions, and knowledge about harassment policies and procedures.